MATTHEW DANTE

Bikers of Mayhem
Book 1

PRIMAL URGES

BIKERS OF MAYHEM
BOOK 1

MATTHEW DANTE

CONTENTS

Primal Urges
(Bikers of Mayhem - Book 1)

Copyright ©2025 Matthew Dante
All rights reserved.
Cover by **The Ravens Touch** @the.ravens.touch
Edited by Steph White (Kat's Literary Services)

This book is a work of fiction. Names, characters, places, and incidents either are products of the author's imagination or are used fictitiously. Any resemblance to actual persons, living or dead, events, or locales is entirely coincidental.

Warning: This book contains scenes of violence, murder, kidnapping and alcohol abuse.

ISBN eBook: 978-1-0689041-4-1

Paperback: 978-1-0689041-3-4

PROLOGUE
LUCAS

The sound of Lucas's heartbeat thumping in his ears was the only sound that filled the space around him.

It had taken on a life of its own.

It was a warning.

A monster.

An omen sent to warn him that what he was about to do was not a wise idea.

The room was silent.

There was no humming from the air conditioner that sat perched in their window.

Normally, the sound was soothing. A reminder that he was not alone in all of this. There was hope. A break from the intense heat that usually plagued the room.

But not tonight.

Tonight, even the air conditioner remained silent.

Another sign that perhaps he was about to make the biggest mistake of his life.

His heartbeat kicked up a notch.

He turned toward the bedroom window.

Even the world around him appeared to have abandoned him.

There was no honking or yelling or screeching from the midnight traffic outside. It was as if the entire world around him had gone silent, quietly slipping away while he wasn't looking, leaving him alone to battle his demon.

Yes, the universe somehow sensed that tonight, something dark and sinister was about to unfold.

Outside, the stars appeared to have lost their brightness, opting instead to dull their lights and turn their faces away from the third-floor walk-up, the setting for tonight's suspenseful thriller.

Lucas swallowed hard as he sat in the darkness... waiting.

He tried to control his breathing, hoping that his courage would not fail him as it had so many times before.

He hated himself for being so weak. He cursed his parents for not raising him to be a tougher man. If they had taught him to stand up for himself and be brave, perhaps he wouldn't be in this mess.

But that was merely something that people in his situation told themselves, no doubt hoping to regain some of the dignity they had lost over the years.

Lucas was weak. And he knew it.

Today alone, he'd changed his mind at least seven times.

Always so weak. He hated himself.

Sitting on the floor, with his knees pulled tight against his chest, he hoped that this time he'd have the courage to do what needed to be done.

He knew that he would never be happy again. He'd resigned himself to that sad truth.

Love was a myth—a cruel joke that some romance author decided to play on a naive and unsuspecting world.

When one really thought about it, love was the cause of so many tragedies. Murder-suicides, broken hearts, even... domestic abuse.

That last one was strange in theory. When someone loves someone, why would they feel the need to hurt that person? But if you ever ask an abuser why they beat or abused their partners, they will always say that they did it because they loved them.

Was it true love? Or just a desire to maintain control?

As he said, "love" was the cause of so many tragedies.

Lucas knew that his outlook on love was grim, but in retrospect, how many atrocities had been committed in the name of love?

The bedroom door swung open, momentarily blinding him as the light from the hallway assaulted his eyes.

Lucas jumped, startled as the door slammed against the wall.

He must have heard that sound a thousand times, yet each time, it was just as terrifying as the first. It wasn't the sound he feared, per se, but rather what came next.

Him.

Stumbling into the bedroom, breath smelling like cheap

whiskey, his once knight in shining armor reached for the door and steadied himself.

"There ya are, you fuckin' prick."

Lucas didn't look up. Instead, he pulled his knees closer to his chest and began counting the seconds until he would receive his first blow. It was always to the cheek.

For some reason, that appeared to be Darryl's signature move. One strong blow to the face, followed by a tug on his arm to pull him to his feet.

Right on cue, the first of many stars flashed across Lucas's eyes as his boyfriend's knuckles greeted his cheekbone.

Lucas fell to the side. Given that he was already huddled on the floor, his body didn't have far to travel.

A large, meaty paw grabbed hold of Lucas's once-soft skin, tightening his grip before yanking him to his feet.

"Why you been hidin'?" the man he had come to loathe snarled before tossing Lucas's body across the room as if he weighed nothing.

His body struck the bed before bouncing off and landing on the hardwood floor—the site of countless scraped knees and sore jaws.

No. Those were not the pains one enjoyed in the throes of passion; those were the pains one suffered when they allowed a monster into their bedroom.

"Come here. Give me those pretty lips," Darryl slurred once again, this time using his free hand to tug Lucas's face toward his manhood.

There had been a period... once upon a time, when Lucas

found all this aggression a massive turn-on. But there was a fine line between macho aggression in the bedroom and full-fledged drunken domestic violence.

This, right here, was the latter.

Lucas struggled against Darryl's pull, knowing that he only had to fight him off for just a few more minutes... *hopefully.*

The sleeping pills he had dumped into his boyfriend's bottle of whiskey should have kicked in by now. He had used triple the recommended dosage, taking into account the massive size of Darryl's body and the hope that the drugs would knock him out as quickly as possible.

Having a boyfriend who was six foot four was hot in theory, but not when that massive body was being used against you... to hurt you, intimidate you, and even prevent you from leaving. Kind of like tonight.

He knew the only way he could ever escape Darryl's clutches was to vanish into the night while the man was unconscious. Thus, the sleeping pills.

While Lucas might hate the man's guts, he also didn't want to kill the abusive bastard.

Cold, wet liquid splashed against Lucas's cheek as Darryl lifted the bottle to his lips to take another heaving sip.

Drink. Drink up, you fucking bastard. I hope that you pass out and smash your goddamn face against that hideous dresser that you bought from one of your fucked-up friends.

He watched as the bottle slowly slipped from his boyfriend's fingers. Lucas smiled. Darryl took an uneasy step backward, nearly losing his balance in the process.

"Wow. That was a trippy... bastar..." Darryl placed his hand on the mattress, attempting to steady himself and regain his commanding position over Lucas's body.

"Come. Boy. Suck my di..."

The words died on his lips.

A second later, Darryl's eyes rolled back in his head, and his giant body came crashing to the floor.

A moment of panic filled Lucas's chest.

What if he really did kill the poor bastard?

No. Evil doesn't die that easily.

It was going to take a lot more than a handful of sleeping pills to end that piece of shit's life.

No. Tonight was about knocking Darryl out long enough for him to grab his packed bag from the linen closet and disappear into the night.

With Darryl being who he was, this was the only way that Lucas could escape.

Well, there was another way, but there was no way in hell he was going down that path.

Holding his breath, Lucas leaned over Darryl's body to see if he could feel any breath against his cheek.

Yup. As suspected, the bastard was still alive.

This was it. There was no turning back now.

Gathering all of his courage, Lucas jumped to his feet and ran into the hallway to grab the *go bag* he had packed earlier in the day. Just a few necessities—some cash, some clothing, his passport—he really wasn't sure where he was running to.

Adrenaline pumping through his veins, all he could hear was the racing beat of his heart in his ears.

This was it. He was finally doing it.

He's going to be so pissed when he wakes up.

Swallowing the lump of fear, Lucas pulled his duffel bag from the linen closet and ran toward the apartment door.

Go! Don't think about it! Just run! It's now or never! Lucas shouted at himself in his head.

He snatched his wallet off the kitchen counter, then shoved his feet into his steel-toed boots.

His heart was pounding so hard; he was amazed that the neighbors hadn't called to complain.

This was it. There was no turning back now. He needed to get the fuck out while he still had the chance... and the courage.

As he pulled open the apartment door, he stole a final glance over his shoulder and gazed at the life he had once thought he wanted.

How had he been so wrong?

Taking a deep breath, he stepped out into the hallway and took off like a bat out of hell.

He would continue to run for the next few days. He needed to get as far away from Los Angeles as humanly possible.

He needed to disappear.

Someplace safe.

Someplace where no one knew him.

1

CADEN

"Three more," the voice of Satan himself announced, trying to be encouraging but only managing to make things even more hopeless.

He couldn't give up.

The man had just turned forty and still lifted weights like he was a fuckin' twenty-five-year-old. This, right now, was a matter of pride. If he didn't finish these last three reps, it would only confirm to him and everyone else standing around them that Marcus—his old-ass boss—was still a beast and could take down any punk-ass young'un who dared to puff out their chest.

To be fair, Caden hadn't puffed out his chest. He'd merely asked if Marcus wanted to hit some weights to burn off some of those cupcakes that Alexis brought into the bar last night. They were so sweet and sugary, he swore he could still feel the excitement rolling around in his mouth.

Plus, he needed to maintain his six-pack abs. Women didn't drool over flab and softness.

Breathing in through his nose, he brought the weights down, then breathed out through his mouth as he pushed the weights up again.

The movement was slow and painful. Talk about getting a nice pump in his chest. He was going to look so ripped after this.

"That a boy. Two more," Marcus encouraged.

I fucking hate you, Caden thought to himself. Why did his boss have to be so goddamn strong?

"Come on, Cade, almost there," Ace, another one of the young bucks, cheered.

Great. Another set of eyes to watch his downfall and humiliation if he didn't finish up the last two reps of his bench press.

He could hear the taunting comments in his mind if he failed.

Can't keep up with the big guy?

Don't worry. One day, you'll be as strong as Big Daddy.

This was now a matter of self-respect.

He took another breath and pushed everything he had into the last two reps. His arms burned, and his lungs felt like they were going to explode from his chest.

"There we go!" he heard his boss cheer as he helped guide the shaky bar back onto the rack.

Huffing, Caden sat up slowly. Sweat dripped down his face.

Stay strong. Don't let them see how much those last two reps nearly killed you.

His boss gave him a slap on the side of the shoulder, then passed him his water bottle.

"Thanks." Caden huffed, trying not to show how out of breath and in pain he really was.

"You did good, man. Your form is looking tight."

Why did his boss always have to be such a fucking nice guy? It made hating him always so damn hard. Not that he really hated his boss. He only hated him when his manhood and pride were at stake. Like right this moment.

"Thanks, boss. You weren't doing too bad yourself."

"For an old man, you mean?" Marcus chuckled.

"Hey, forty is not old," Caden rushed to clarify. He didn't want his boss to think that he didn't respect him or that he thought being forty was old.

"Well, from what I hear, being old starts at thirty-two, or even late twenties, like that little prick over there," he said, nodding over his shoulder at Ace, who was busy checking out some dude as he bent over to pick up a dumbbell.

"Hey, there's nothing little about my prick," Ace defended, snapping his head around and glaring at them both.

Marcus and Caden burst out laughing.

"Hey, don't get all defensive. I'm sure it's well-proportioned for a guy your size," Caden joked.

Ace was five-ten, but standing next to both Caden and Marcus, who were six-two and six-four, the man looked like he belonged in munchkin land.

Marcus wrapped his massive arm around Ace's shoulders and pulled him in for a headlock. He rubbed his knuckle through the guy's hair, smiling as Ace shouted and fought back against his attacker.

Caden couldn't help but laugh. Watching Marcus and Ace together made him wish he had siblings as well. Marcus and Ace were brothers. Well, stepbrothers, if you want to get technical.

Marcus's father remarried Ace's mother when Marcus was sixteen and Ace was three. Marcus practically raised Ace when it became clear that both of their parents preferred to drink and party rather than spend time raising and taking care of their children.

When Marcus's assault on Ace's hair finally finished, he released his brother and patted him on the back.

"So, tell us about how your hot date went last night?" Marcus asked, removing the small weights from Cade's bench press and adding a heavier plate on both ends.

Fuck, he better not expect him to do another set at a heavier weight.

Marcus must have seen the look on Cade's face because he chuckled.

"The weights are for me. Figured I'd get in one more set before calling it a day."

The grip on Cade's stomach loosened. He would be able to lift his arms after all.

"So? Date? How'd it go?" Marcus asked, glancing over at his younger brother.

Ace crossed his arms against his chest, appearing suddenly pissed.

"Well, the date started off great and strong until he found out who my brother was. Then he suddenly remembered that he had to take his sick grandmother to a doctor's appointment."

"At nine o'clock at night?" Marcus asked, pissed that someone would run out on his little brother.

Ace shrugged. "It's always the same. Cockblocked by my own stupid brother."

Cade wondered if Ace truly felt that way or if he was trying to tease his older brother. Marcus had a bit of a reputation in town, so it wouldn't be surprising if guys kept their distance from the boss's younger brother. That was one heart that wouldn't be safe to break.

"Don't be mad. I'm just making sure that you hold out for someone who's worthy of that ass of yours."

Ace's mouth dropped open.

"What makes you think I'm a bottom?"

He totally was.

Marcus and Cade both gave Ace a "who do you think you're kidding" look.

Rolling his eyes, Ace gave them both the finger. "You're both assholes."

Cade chuckled as he positioned himself at the top of the bench press, readying himself to give his boss a spot.

Marcus slid down on the bench press. "But you love us anyway," Marcus added as he lifted the bar into the air.

"Don't forget to wipe down the bench after you're done.

Not sure if crabs can leak through sweaty gym shorts, but it's best to be safe, just in case. Right, Marcus?" Ace cut as he picked up his gear and headed toward the locker room.

Cade couldn't help but laugh at Ace's ruthlessness. There was a reason that he loved the little homo.

Below him, Marcus shook his head back and forth. "I don't have crabs."

"Sure you don't, boss."

2

CADEN

*S*tanding outside the bar, Caden watched as some dude made out with his girl while sitting on his Harley. It wasn't an uncommon sight. Some rough-around-the-edges biker dude, getting his face swallowed by some pretty little thing with long black hair, tattoos up and down her arms, and a miniskirt that introduced the world to her vagina.

Ride 'em Hard was the name of the bar.

It was the bar of choice for those who lived a little more on the... *wild side*. Mostly, it was bikers, gang members, and newly divorced women—and a few men—looking to let loose and take a little ride on the untamed, rougher side of the testosterone pool. Perhaps hook up with someone in one of the less-than-desirable bathrooms or receive sloppy head out back where people pretended nothing happened.

Caden loved it here.

Officially, he worked as a bouncer, making sure that

everyone followed the rules and things didn't get too rowdy or too out of hand. There had to be a bit of excitement, or people would not continue to return.

Mostly, Cade stood around, looking ripped and menacing. It wasn't very often that he had to crack open skulls or take people out back and introduce them to the pavement. But when people misbehaved, Caden had no issues getting a little blood on his boots.

Not many caused trouble though. Most people were too afraid of Marcus to disrespect him or his place of business.

His boss had a bit of a *reputation*.

Everyone knew that Marcus earned a living doing things that would most likely earn people a VIP ticket straight to the fiery gates of hell. They all enjoyed partying with him but knew better than to get on his bad side. That was how people disappeared.

But Cade didn't judge.

It wasn't like he was a saint himself and hadn't done things that might make others cringe or pass judgment.

When all was said and done, he, along with all his fellow coworkers, would be partying it up in hell right next to their boss and fearless leader.

Even if the tank could still outbench him any day of the week…

In addition to owning Ride 'em Hard, Marcus was also the leader of the *Shadow Vipers*, a motorcycle gang that dabbled in drugs, weapons, and rare antiquities. Basically, Marcus and his crew could get anyone, anything… for a price, of course.

It was this knowledge that Marcus was the leader of a biker gang that kept people shaking in their boots.

Caden was also a member of the Shadow Vipers—the same as most of the guys who worked at Ride 'em Hard. Being a bouncer at the bar was what Caden reported to Uncle Sam. The rest of his income came from crew business.

"How's it lookin'?" a voice asked, sneaking up behind him.

He turned his head slightly and gave his buddy Nikolai an up nod with his head. He was still fixed on the amateur porn shoot taking place just steps away from where he stood.

"It's good. Just watching *Daddy Bear* over there get his face licked off by *Princess Peach*."

A guttural moan escaped Nikolai's throat.

"Fuck, that piece looks nice and juicy."

Caden wasn't sure which person his buddy was referring to. He'd heard rumors that perhaps Nikolai liked to take it both ways, but was never able to confirm whether the man ever took dick or not. He knew that the man was notorious for participating in three ways, but he never really got into the "who stuck what where" part of the stories. He would just randomly make generic comments like the one he just made, leaving everyone to guess and speculate.

Not that Caden had an issue if the giant beefy Russian was bi. If anything, he pitied the man... or woman who had to take his Russian piece of meat. He'd seen what the guy was packing, and let's just say god used double the amount of clay when he was sculpting his junk.

"Tell me about it," Caden agreed. "How are things going inside?"

Nikolai took his position on the other side of the entrance and folded his arms across his chest. If the man wasn't intimidating before, he definitely looked like he enjoyed eating puppies for breakfast and scaring young children for fun.

Having two big, scary-looking dudes manning the entrance was great for business. It gave the place that rough, bad-boy feel while telling the world that they didn't put up with bullshit.

Tearing his eyes away from the two fornicating on the motorcycle before them, Nikolai nodded over his shoulder.

"Had to break up a fight between Eddie and Dusty, then had to remind *Thelma and Louise* that their tits had to stay inside their shirts even when dancing at the back of the bar."

Thelma and Louise were two middle-aged women who began coming to the bar when they both left their husbands five years ago. The crew referred to them as *Thelma and Louise* because of how they dressed and acted. They always came in wearing the tiniest miniskirts and cowboy boots. They were a lively duo who enjoyed teasing the men in the bar and occasionally going down on them when they were feeling horny.

But piss them off, and you were done for.

Marcus had set up a jukebox at the back of the bar that played some rock and heavy metal. He even added a Taylor Swift album in case any of the *rainbow crew* decided to give the bar a go.

Ace was openly gay. Occasionally, he'd bring in a friend or two who usually sat nervously in the corner while a bar full of drunken biker men and women watched them with curiosity.

Everybody knew that Ace was Marcus's little brother, so nobody would ever dare say a word to him about being gay, but occasionally, they did get the bigoted traveler who stopped in for a beer and decided to run their mouth. They usually left the bar with a fat lip and matching black eyes.

None of Marcus's crew would ever allow one of their own to be disrespected, be he gay, straight, bi, or other. There was a certain code that they all lived by, and standing up for one another was part of that code.

They were the Shadow Vipers. Nobody messed with their family.

"You going to be alright out here? I'm going to head inside and take a leak."

Nikolai nodded, turning his attention back to the princess who was grinding her cooch up against her man with such intensity Caden was surprised it hadn't burst into flames.

At least someone was taking advantage of the opportunity to get themselves off.

Making his way through the bar, Cade nodded at regulars and patted guys on the back as he passed them by.

It was a Saturday night, so the place was packed to the rafters.

They lived in a small town called Baton, just outside of Roswell, New Mexico. The population was less than twenty-five thousand and hadn't even found itself a place on the map.

Other than drinking and fucking, there wasn't much else to do in the small podunk town. Teens seemed to love the movie theater, but mostly, it showed films that had already come out on DVD. The town wasn't too concerned with keeping up with the rest of the world around it, it seemed. It had its charm, but mostly, people lived there to be left alone.

The town had one sheriff, a man by the name of Sheriff Burke, who basically only got off his ass when there was a fire or some traveling tourist decided to run their mouth and had two of their teeth punched in. Locals didn't take kindly to people running their lips or thinking that they were better than them.

Truth be told, the order of the town was mostly maintained by Marcus and his crew—crew being the guys who stood behind Marcus and most of whom worked at this very bar. There were a few guys and girls who did other work for Marcus, but the majority of the crew was stationed at Ride 'em Hard.

Stepping up to the urinal, Caden unzipped his fly and pulled out his cock. He let out a sigh as his bladder began to empty.

He'd been needing to take a piss for the past forty-five minutes, but Nikolai had been busy doing *God knows what* inside the bar. He didn't dare leave the door unmanned, especially on a Saturday night. You never knew what drunken idiot might stumble in—or out—of the bar, causing trouble that would reflect badly on Marcus and the rest of the crew.

It was just safer for everyone if he held his dick like a grown man.

Shaking himself off, he tucked his dick back into his jeans and washed his hands in the sink.

Glancing up at the water-stained mirror, he fixed his hair and adjusted his shirt. The fabric stretched tightly around his swollen muscles, making his biceps look huge and firm. Ladies liked a man with big, strong arms.

Deciding that he looked decent enough to catch the eye of one or two horny chicks, he adjusted his package and tried to remember if he replaced the condoms in his wallet. He always made sure he had at least two on him at all times, just in case his lay wanted to bring a friend.

He needed to get laid.

He hadn't busted a nut in the last three days, and he was starting to get a little edgy. Walking around a biker bar with a semi was great for the ladies but not so great for the dudes.

"Don't worry, little guy. We'll get you some attention tonight," Caden said to his reflection before reaching for the door and stepping out into the hallway.

It happened so fast that Caden barely had any time to react.

A tray of empty glasses went flying into the air as some tiny thing dressed in a tight black shirt barreled into Caden's right side.

Without thinking, Caden reached out and caught the scraggly frame before it had a chance to crash into the wall across from them.

The tray and glasses were left to their own fate and crashed to the floor with a wondrous roar.

Cheers and laughter erupted from the bar as witnesses to the tragic collision expressed their enthusiasm for the violence and chaos that had unfolded right before them.

"Shit!" the startled young man gasped, grabbing hold of Caden and abandoning his duties as *guardian of the tray*.

"Whoa," Caden exclaimed, pulling the young man into his chest in a gesture that could only be described as "protective lover."

"Oh! Umm, I'm sorry," the bashful young man exclaimed, glancing up at Caden with wide eyes and an expression of terror.

His solid brown eyes resembled those of a deer who had just come face-to-face with a lion out in the open. There was a look of fear and panic and momentary loss of motor function.

"I... I... didn't mean to bump into you," the boy finally choked out once his brain appeared to recalculate.

The mysterious young man straightened up and peeled himself away from Cade's muscular frame.

The boy looked terrified. It wasn't his fault, yet the kid was acting like he had just murdered his goldfish.

Caden felt horrible. He reached out and placed his hand on the kid's shoulder.

"Hey, hey. It's alright, kid. It was my fault for not making sure the coast was clear before barreling out of the washroom like that. I've never been a graceful guy."

A tiny smile tugged at the corners of the boy's lips.

Caden was pretty sure he was just about to get a smile when...

The boy gazed down at the carnage at their feet.

Shattered glass, leftover beer, and whiskey were strewn together like a last-minute Irish afterparty on St. Paddy's Day.

"Shit. Shit. I'm such a screwup! I'm going to get my stupid ass fired."

Before Caden could say a word, the boy dropped to his knees and began picking up the shards of broken glass and tossing them back onto the tray he'd been carrying.

What was up with this kid? It was just a couple of broken pint glasses.

Joining the boy on his knees, Caden began helping the kid clean up the mess before someone accidentally stepped on a piece and complained that they now had to have their foot amputated.

Nothing like a big, burly, tough guy getting a baby cut to make the world suddenly come to a crashing halt.

"Don't worry about it, kid. This place probably loses about twenty glasses a week. Who knew that being drunk could make people so clumsy?"

A soft chuckle escaped from the boy. He looked up at Cade but quickly glanced away when he noticed that Cade was already staring at him.

The boy blushed.

"Yeah, well, this isn't the first tray of glasses that I've completely destroyed tonight. At this rate, people are going to be drinking out of soup bowls by the end of the night."

"Nope. Not possible," Cade refuted. The boy looked up at him, perplexed. "We don't serve soup here, so no soup bowls. Dinner plates, perhaps, but I wouldn't recommend them for holding volumes of liquid. Another recipe for disaster."

The boy chuckled again. His face seemed to relax, and most of the tension had disappeared from his shoulders.

Perfect. Now he didn't need to worry about him accidentally dying of nervousness.

"I take it you're new here?" Caden asked, motioning to Alexis, the bartender, to bring them a broom. Why they were using their hands to pick up shards of glass was beyond him.

"Yeah. First night on the job." The boy was back to concentrating on cleaning his mess and was barely aware that Caden was still talking.

"And they decided it was a good idea to start you on one of the busiest nights of the week?" Caden asked, kind of surprised that Marcus would make such a rookie mistake.

"I might have lied and said that I had previous busboy experience."

Oh, that made sense. Lying to the boss was never a smart move.

"Here," Alexis said, passing Caden a broom before rushing back behind the bar. The bar was busy, and there were only two bartenders working the bar that night.

"Here, stand up." Caden reached down and pulled the boy up by his underarms. "Let me."

He began sweeping up the remaining pieces of broken glass before collecting them into the dustpan. The cleanup only took two minutes, but with the way the boy was nervously looking over his shoulder, it felt like an eternity.

The kid really was a bundle of nerves.

"There. All done," Caden announced with a hint of pride in his voice.

It wasn't that he felt a sense of accomplishment for sweeping the floor; it was more of a sense of pleasure at having fixed the young man's problem for him. He wasn't sure why, but the kid seemed overly nervous and was taking this breaking of some glasses way too personally.

"Thanks, mister." The boy was back to looking at his feet. It was like he was intimidated or uncomfortable with making eye contact with people, or perhaps he was just uncomfortable with him.

"It's Caden. But everyone here calls me Cade." He extended his hand and waited for the boy to introduce himself.

"Nice to meet you, Cade. I'm Lucas." The boy glanced up and made eye contact only for a moment before looking back down at the floor.

Jesus. Who was this guy? The guy was going to get eaten alive by the customers of this bar if he didn't grow a pair and stop being so... shy?

"Nice to meet you, too, buddy. Let me know if you need anything else. I'm one of the bouncers here at the bar."

"I know," Lucas said, catching Caden a little off guard.

He knew he was a bouncer?

Lucas reached for the dustpan and picked up the discarded tray.

"Thanks again for the help, mister." He glanced up quickly before disappearing down the hallway toward the makeshift kitchen Marcus had upgraded a few summers ago.

Watching him disappear into the darkness, Caden wasn't quite sure how he felt about their newest addition. There was something sweet and endearing about the awkwardness and shyness of the boy. But to be honest, that sort of personality was going to get trampled by the animals who came drinking at the bar.

He guessed he would have to see how the boy handled himself.

Caden turned and headed back toward the door, wondering if the porn shoot was still taking place.

3

LUCAS

*I*t was just after three thirty a.m. when Lucas climbed the squeaky old ladder that led up to the loft he now called home. It wasn't much. Basically, it was a large open space at the top of a barn that Old Man Benson had converted into living quarters.

There was a tiny bathroom and shower that Benson had installed on the main level, with a bed and living space up in the barn rafters. The place was... quaint. Not something Lucas had ever envisioned himself living in, but hey, he needed to do what he needed to do, even if it was only for a few months.

He was broke and needed to save up cash so that he could find a much better place to live. But for now, Mr. Benson's barn loft would have to do. Plus, it might be difficult to rent a place without doing a credit and criminal check. He couldn't afford the additional risk.

Stripping off his clothes, he turned on the water in the

shower and stepped inside. The water was cold, turning luke-warm only after rotating the faucet as far to the left as possible and waiting a few minutes.

Fuck his life.

Grabbing the bar of soap, he rubbed it between his hands, working up a nice lather as he waited for the water to heat up.

It's a roof over your head. It will do for the time being.

He hated his life. How had he gotten to this point? Alone. In a strange town. Broke and constantly looking over his shoulder.

He had once been happy.

On his way to having a promising career, having graduated from college with a degree in musical theater. He'd even started auditioning for a few musicals that he hoped would land him his first role on stage and under the spotlight for thousands of adoring fans.

But none of that had happened. Instead, he met... *him*.

Lucas tucked his head under the spray and let the promising warm water run over his body.

It felt good, like being wrapped in a warm embrace.

Safe and secure.

Lucas had once felt safe and secure. Wrapped in *his* powerful, warm arms...

Once.

It had started like something out of a movie. A romance, made-for-TV kind of movie. Not a blockbuster hit, but something that left you feeling all warm and tingly.

But then, somehow, it all went wrong...

Standing at the end of the Santa Monica Pier, Lucas raised his face toward the sky and let the warm California sun drip over his nose and cheeks.

God, he loved the heat.

He was a Cali boy. Born and raised. He had just graduated from college and was excited to finally be able to start auditioning for roles in musicals that were about to open. If he worked really hard, he hoped that in a year or two, he would be able to land the starring role in one of LA's biggest musicals. A few years after that, he hoped to get enough credits and work experience to land him a role in one of the major musicals playing in New York and then eventually move on to London, England.

That was his dream. To become world-famous and perform in London's famous West End. Perhaps even conduct a performance or two in William Shakespeare's Globe Theatre. What a dream that would be.

Lowering his head, he took one last look over the Pacific Ocean and smiled. The world was his to conquer.

Reaching for the cache of shopping bags he had nestled by his feet, he winced when the bags were suddenly torn from his hand.

What the fuck? *Lucas thought to himself, startled.*

He looked up just in time to see a man with dark-orange hair dash down the pier, clutching the bags filled with end-of-school clothing that he had just purchased as a graduation gift to himself.

"Hey! Thief! Stop! Stop him!" Lucas shouted, knowing full well there was no point in yelling. Not one single person was

going to stop what they were doing in order to help him catch his robber.

Lo and behold, he was right. Not one single person looked up or reacted to his pleas for help.

Seriously. What was the world coming to?

Lucas watched as the man got about halfway up the pier before he slowed, trying to blend in with those power walking around him.

"Great," Lucas whispered, wondering how long it would take him to save up enough money to replace all the clothing the man had just stolen.

Further up the pier, a tall man with a buzz cut and a chiseled jaw glanced over at Lucas before turning his head toward the thief himself.

To Lucas's surprise, the man took off after the thief, tackling him to the ground at the top of the pier.

Lucas watched in amazement as the man struggled with the thief, giving him two powerful punches to the face. The thief stopped struggling and dropped the bags from his grip. He covered his nose with his hands and rolled onto his side in pain.

The modern-day Captain America got off the cowering thief and gathered the stolen bags he had dropped.

Slowly, the mystery man began making his way back to where Lucas was standing, shocked and even a little impressed.

It wasn't every day that a six-foot-four hunk of man-beef stepped in and came to his rescue.

"Are you okay?" the man asked once he reached Lucas at the bottom of the pier.

He set the bags down by his feet and placed a gentle hand on Lucas's shoulder.

The man's touch was incredible—both strong and gentle, like a Disney prince who had come to his rescue.

"Did he hurt you?" the man asked, his chestnut eyes analyzing every inch of Lucas's face, no doubt searching for signs of injury or trauma.

Swoon.

The man's eyes were breathtaking and heart-stopping.

Was it possible for someone to be able to see into your soul and know exactly what it was that you needed?

At that moment, he needed a protector and a compassionate man.

"No. I'm fine. A little shaken, but fine."

Staring at the tall and solid man, the first thought that entered Lucas's mind was hero. *How many people can say that they had a gorgeous man come running to their rescue and tackle their attacker?*

If this were a rom-com, it would be the meet-cute that everyone talked about.

"Big, strong man comes to quirky man's rescue," the caption would read.

"Still, you should probably get yourself checked out by a doctor. What if you have a concussion or whiplash or something? We can't have a cute guy like you suddenly falling or passing out on his way home."

Cute guy?

Lucas blushed. He wasn't used to hot men calling him cute.

If someone were to ask him what his ideal type of man was,

31

it would undoubtedly be the man standing right in front of him.

Tall, dark, and courageous. Willing to take care of him and ready to jump in to defend the man he loves.

Could his dick get any harder?

As if the mystery man somehow sensed his dirty thoughts, the man gave him a cocky smirk.

"I'm Darryl," *his savior announced, raising his hand toward Lucas's.*

"I'm Lucas."

They both smiled, temporarily lost in each other's eyes.

Yup, he was definitely falling for this hunky specimen of a man.

"Thank you for saving my bags. You really are a hero."

Darryl smiled. His teeth were white and perfect, undoubtedly the result of excellent oral hygiene and regular visits to the dentist.

Standing there, with the sun beating down on their faces, Lucas couldn't help but notice... something. Something just behind the dazzling chestnut eyes of his newest favorite hero. Something...

Was it cockiness?

There was something about the way that Darryl was looking at him... like he knew that Lucas was weak and basically ready to lie down and spread his legs for him.

Take me now, you massive stud. Have me any which way you want me.

Perhaps Darryl was sensing his enormous attraction to him. That would make any man cocky as shit.

"It's not every day that I get to rescue such a sexy-looking guy," Darryl noted, giving Lucas a slow once-over, which, of course, ended with a smug smirk.

Yeah, the guy definitely knew how to flirt.

"Now. As your hero, I insist that you let me take you to lunch. A traumatic experience like that deserves a drink or two."

Lucas's face lit up. He would gladly do just about anything if Darryl asked him to. His hormones were racing, and the man appeared to be the embodiment of every sexual fantasy he ever had since puberty.

"Well, how can I refuse such a charming man?"

Picking up Lucas's bags, Darryl took his hand in his and began leading him up the pier toward the spot where a police officer was placing the would-be thief in handcuffs.

They spent the next six hours enjoying food and drinks while discussing their past experiences with the art of love. It seemed that neither had been very lucky in that department.

It was just after eight in the evening when Darryl escorted Lucas back to his tiny apartment, where he proceeded to spend the next three hours giving him orgasm after orgasm.

A hero's work was never done.

Placing his head back under the running water, Lucas wondered why he hadn't noticed the warning signs earlier.

Would things have been different? Would he have been able to escape much sooner?

He wasn't sure.

But that was the past. This was his future.

A chance to start anew.

No one knew him here. He hoped that, given the small population of Baton, it might be a place where Darryl wouldn't think to look.

Running the lathered soap across his body, his hand landed on his cock. One person's face appeared before him.

Cade.

The man was sex on a stick. His body was chiseled, and his biceps were the size of Lucas's head. Okay, he might be exaggerating, but his muscles were sexy as fuck.

He definitely had a type.

Big, strong, testosterone-fueled, and a protector. Hell, even Caden's biker-dude beard made Lucas hard as fuck. He could only imagine how good that facial hair must feel being dragged across his inner thighs.

Lucas didn't want to think about how similar Cade was to his ex. His physical size and dominance, even the way he looked at him with dangerous eyes. It was both sexy as hell and scary as fuck.

He'd spotted Cade at the beginning of his shift but lost track of him once the herd of drunken patrons began stumbling in. He had been so distracted running around all night that he hadn't even noticed when the bathroom door swung open and the solid wall of muscle stepped out.

Smashing into Cade's muscular frame was like smashing into a Mack truck. He swore he practically bounced off the guy, only to be stunned when the smoking-hot bouncer reached out and caught him.

Pulling him into those big protective arms, Lucas just

about died. He wanted to spend the rest of his life nestled in between those bulging, hot cannons.

Breathing in Cade's masculine scent, Lucas was surprised that the man didn't jump back when his cock quickly thickened.

Speaking of cocks, Lucas began rubbing long strokes on his own. Memories of Caden pressed firmly against him had his brain and dick in horny-man overload.

When their eyes locked together, Lucas swore he felt a zap of lust shoot from his balls all the way up to the tip of his cock.

If only that man wasn't straight.

Lucas would have loved to drop to his knees and swallow that rod all the way down to the base. Show that burly bouncer just how good of a cocksucker he really was.

Yup, Lucas had a type.

Fucking his fist, he closed his eyes and tried to imagine the beefy rough bouncer... alone... naked... and waiting for him on his bed.

Cade was the type of guy you knew had to have the perfect cock. His size would be above average, the girth just thick enough to stretch you out without causing pain, and, of course, he would have the most perfectly shaped mushroom head on his dick.

Guys like Caden got any girls they wanted. He was confident, strong, and sexy as hell.

The moment he saw Caden, he knew he had to keep his distance. He didn't have the greatest track record when it came to falling for men.

Still, he could only imagine how great Caden's cock must taste.

Leaning his head against the shower tiles, Lucas picked up the pace, moaning as he jerked himself with purpose.

He imagined taking all of Caden's cock down his throat, gagging and slobbering, feeling it harden in his mouth as he got closer to busting.

Lucas couldn't hold off any longer. He felt his balls tighten moments before shooting his load all over the shower wall.

His legs shivered, and his body spasmed, but none of that mattered as he imagined himself swallowing down every last drop of Caden's warm load.

Once the fog cleared from his brain, Lucas realized that the water had once again turned cold.

He splashed water onto the wall, watching as his cum slid down the tile and disappeared into the drain below.

He shivered.

It was time to get his ass into bed.

Lucas reached for the towel as he stepped out of the tub.

He needed to forget about Cade. Fucking around with a straight boy never led to anything good.

The last thing he needed at the moment was trouble.

4

CADEN

Sunday afternoons at Ride 'em Hard were always dead. Most people were too busy nursing their Saturday night hangovers to even consider slinking their way back into the dingy biker bar.

Cade didn't mind. He got paid for doing easy work. Usually, Marcus got the team to work on remedial tasks that hadn't gotten done during the week or used the time to discuss *other* crew business. So it wasn't any surprise when Marcus asked them all to gather at the center of the bar shortly after three.

"Afternoon, assholes. Glad to see you're all still standing and not whining about your little headaches or why your knees hurt when you bend them." Marcus turned a knowing eye toward Damian, who was sitting in a booth with a hand on his forehead. Damian straightened up when he realized that Marcus was talking about him.

"Hey, I'm not whining. Just massaging my head,"

Damian explained, trying to reclaim the balls he once had before he decided to go shot-for-shot with Big Al, one of the locals who ran the town's auto shop, last night.

Big Al was six-four and three hundred pounds, while Damian was a meager five-ten, one hundred and sixty pounds. It was no wonder that the man got his ass handed to him.

"Massaging your head, licking your wounds. Either way, you got your ass pummeled by Big Al last night. I'm amazed you're still able to sit with the pounding he gave you."

The group around them chuckled.

Damian gave his boss the finger.

"Love you too." Marcus blew him an air kiss. "Next, I wanted to officially welcome Lucas Braden to the team." Marcus motioned for Lucas to step forward, then put his arm around the boy when he approached.

The size difference was comical. Marcus was a towering six foot four, while Lucas was a petite five-eight. It was like staring at David and Goliath or a bodybuilding porn star and his newby twink scene partner. There was no doubt in Cade's mind that if the two of them were ever to fuck, the boy would be torn in two.

Lucas raised a shy hand and waved. He glanced around at all his new coworkers before his gaze settled on Cade. They both stared at each other for a lingering moment before Lucas eventually called chicken and diverted his eyes.

"Lucas is new in town and will be working here as a busboy, cleaning off tables and helping Alexis at the bar. I want everyone to make Lucas feel welcome and show him how things are done around here. Any questions?"

"Yeah. Where are you from?" Ace asked, taking a step forward and crossing his arms against his chest.

Ace was not like most of the other members of the Shadow Vipers. He was slim and smaller in stature and always smiling even when customers were being dicks.

It was sickening, really. How could one person be so goddamn cheery all day, every day? Perhaps, he was popping some happy pills when no one was looking... or maybe he was getting some really good dick on the side. It's amazing what taking a thick eight-incher will do for a person's mood, or so he was told.

But whatever the cause, he couldn't help but love the little piece of shit.

Lucas's eyes darted around the room, looking like a scared little bunny that had just been surrounded by a pack of coyotes.

"I... I..."

Why did he look so nervous?

"I'm from the West Coast," Lucas finally managed.

Okay. Vague much?

Caden leaned back with his ass pressed up against the table. He studied their newest addition.

The boy was slim and clean-cut, with light-brown hair that was neatly styled. He wasn't like the rest of them. He didn't exude confidence or give off that bad-boy vibe. He wasn't covered in tattoos—not that Cade could see, anyway —and he didn't strut around like he owned the world.

Instead, he appeared shy and nervous and definitely uncomfortable being gawked at by a room full of testosterone-fueled men who pumped iron and were addicted to inking their bodies.

If the guy was so uncomfortable around rough-looking dudes, why was he working at a biker bar?

Ace continued to gawk at Lucas, confused and clearly wondering if he should follow up with another question or just let things go. Ace was a talker and enjoyed getting to know people.

Not being able to converse with someone who fascinated him must be driving Ace crazy.

Caden tried not to laugh at Ace. The boy had issues.

Marcus placed a hand on Lucas's shoulder, no doubt sensing the discomfort emanating from the boy.

"It doesn't matter where he's from or what brought him to this shithole we call home. What matters is that he is here now and part of our brotherhood. The Shadow Vipers take care of their family, so we are all going to look after him and make sure that he settles in nicely."

Caden smiled.

That was one of the things he loved about his boss. The man knew when to back off and when to give people their space. He was their leader, their protector, and also their friend.

While their crew might be filled with intimidating-looking men, deep down, they all cared for one another.

The Shadow Vipers were a big, messed-up family who

always had each other's backs—even when they were being vague and shifty as hell.

"That's enough lovey-dovey bullshit for one day," Marcus continued. "Get your asses back to work and make me some money."

Around the room, people mumbled curses and made sarcastic comments as they all moseyed back to their assigned duties. They all loved their boss and fearless leader, but they also had images to protect. Feigning protest was one way that they could all pretend that they had the balls to actually stand up to their boss.

"Tough, macho biker who sucks boss's dick" did not have the same effect as "smart-ass tough guy who doesn't let anyone tell him what to do."

One scenario would get you laid; the other would make you some man's bitch in a federal penitentiary.

Yes, that was what they all told themselves, but deep down, they all knew that if it came down to it, they would all get down on their knees and open wide if Marcus asked.

Sunday nights were never busy at the bar. That meant that Caden and Nikolai could alternate working the Sunday shift. They didn't need two bouncers working the door, so Cade was free to hang out inside the bar most of the evening, helping with various tasks.

"So, what do you think about our newest addition?"

Cade asked Alexis, who was wiping out the inside of a pint glass.

She glanced over at Lucas, who was trying to hang a dartboard that had fallen at some point during last night's *battle of the drunken dart masters.*

Looking all masterful and determined, Lucas held a hammer in one hand, a nail in his mouth, and was propping the dartboard up against the wall with his other hand.

"How long do you think it will take him to realize he needs another hand to hammer the nail into the wall?" Cade asked, amused by the hopelessness of their newest addition.

"Yeah. He does look a little lost, doesn't he?"

They both watched as Lucas fumbled around, trying to balance both items while attempting to grab the nail out of his mouth with the hand holding the hammer.

The boy looked confused.

"You may want to go give the kid a hand before he hurts himself," she added, still watching him struggle.

Cade let out a snort before straightening up and making his way to the back of the bar.

"Having trouble, sweet cheeks?" Caden asked as he stepped up behind the boy.

"Huh? Wh-what?" Lucas asked, startled and nearly dropping the items he'd been carefully balancing.

"Looks like you could use a hand."

Blushing, Lucas lowered the dartboard and held the hammer out to Caden.

"Know how to use one of these?" Lucas asked, looking all cute and innocent.

Something about the boy made Cade want to take the hammer and build him something. He usually felt this way when he was trying to impress a woman with his superior man skills and capabilities.

Caden chuckled.

"Yeah, I think I know my way around a hammer." He took the tool and held out his hand, waiting for Lucas to give him the nail.

The boy just stood there staring at his palm.

Cade tried not to laugh. The boy really was hopeless when it came to fixing things.

"It works better if you give me the nail as well."

"Oh! Shit, sorry," Lucas rushed, his face quickly turning a deeper shade of red before dropping the nail in Caden's massive paw.

"No worries. You're a little bit uptight, aren't you?" Caden asked, turning to face the wall and trying to visually judge where the dartboard should be hung.

He didn't need a measuring tape or level because... well, hey, he was a guy and had a penis.

No self-respecting man needed assistance from some pansy-ass construction tool.

Yes, he was raised in a world where toxic masculinity still ruled. Add that to the expectation that all male bikers be rough and tough men, and Caden did his best to live up to those expectations.

From the corner of his eye, Lucas shrugged his shoulders but didn't say a word.

After double-checking his position on the wall, Caden

placed the nail in its proper position and gave it a few taps with the hammer before giving it a stronger whack. The nail went in perfectly, protruding just enough to hang the board.

He turned and took the dartboard from Lucas.

"There. How does that look?" he asked, adjusting the dartboard before taking a step back and admiring his handiwork.

He felt a swell of pride in his chest.

Man one. Dartboard zero.

"Wow, looks perfect!" Lucas cheered, his face brightening with a smile that could win over a room full of cobras.

Wow, that smile was intoxicating.

It was nice seeing Lucas's face light up. He was kind of cute when he wasn't all nervous and looking like he was about to get eaten by a mountain lion—which made Cade wonder, once again, why someone as shy as Lucas would choose to work at a rough place like this.

The boy looked like he belonged in a coffee shop or perhaps a pet store where he could play with fuzzy animals and give them kisses all day long. Ride 'em Hard didn't exactly seem like the right fit for the boy.

Cade glanced around at the array of tools spread out on the pool table. He hoped that Lucas hadn't attempted to hang the dartboard with a screwdriver or a wrench. However, considering the hopeless look in the guy's eye when he first approached, he very well could have.

"So, is there anything else that needs fixing?" Cade asked, taking a final look around the space.

"Nah. I think Marcus was testing me, trying to figure out exactly what my skill set is and where I truly belong," Lucas said, offering him a half smile.

Over Lucas's shoulder, Cade spotted Marcus talking to Ace but watching the two of them. It wasn't like Marcus to be so petty.

"No. Marcus isn't like that. He asked you to fix this because it needed fixing. He might come across as all mean and angry, but deep down, he really is just a big fluffy love ball."

Lucas chuckled, lowering his gaze.

It was a shame that the boy didn't have more confidence when speaking with others. His smile alone could warm a room.

"Don't tell the boss I said that. Otherwise, he'll have me scrubbing toilets for a month," Caden joked, leaning in closer and breathing in the boy's scent.

He kind of smelled like cherry blossoms—or what he had been told cherry blossoms would smell like because, once again, he had balls.

They both chuckled.

"Well, I guess this is the second time that you've come to my rescue," Lucas noted.

"Yeah, well, let's keep that between us. I have a reputation to maintain. Let's just say that fear and intimidation make working as a bouncer much easier when trying to keep guys in line."

"Given the size of your arms, I'm sure you will always be

intimidating." The boy's eyes widened, and his cheeks flushed when he realized what he had just said. "Your secret's safe with me," he quickly added before making his way around the pool table and throwing the extra tools back into the tool case used by the bar for minor repairs.

Bending over the pool table, Lucas's shirt rode up, exposing a tiny bit of flesh on his lower back and just a hint of tiny butt crack.

Caden stared at Lucas's exposed skin and wondered what it would feel like to grab the boy by the hips and fuck him hard, bent over the pool table.

What was that?

Caden took a step back, his heart pounding in his chest.

He'd never once fantasized about fucking another dude!

Sure, he could admit when a guy was good-looking or physically attractive, but he never once thought about caressing a man's skin or dragging his fingers along another man's pouty red lips.

Whoa! What the fuck was happening?

He was straight and had never before wondered such things.

Suddenly, he felt nervous.

What's going on?

"Umm, I should probably get back to my post," Caden rushed without looking up at the boy. He was too afraid that Lucas might see all of the dirty thoughts currently racing through his brain.

Dirty, rough, and nasty things.

He tried to swallow, but his mouth was suddenly bone dry. He needed to get out of there.

Before his thoughts had another chance to ambush him, he rushed toward the front door as quickly as possible.

5

CADEN

Seventeen Years Ago

"*Caden!*" *his father's voice boomed from the living room. "Get your ass out here!"*

Letting out a huff, Caden slammed his textbook shut and jumped off his bed. This was the third time in an hour his old man had asked for his assistance. There was no way he was going to get this last chapter read before he passed out on his bed from exhaustion.

It was almost midnight, and he had been doing that head-bob thing you do when your eyes fall shut and your head suddenly weighs a thousand pounds. He swore the last time he nearly snapped his neck when his head suddenly fell forward.

Oh well. It was just another assignment that he wasn't going to get done. What were his teachers going to do? Fail him? Schools weren't allowed to fail students anymore. Something about it hurting their self-esteem or something.

48

Not like being stupid and not knowing the basics of math and science ever hurt one's self-esteem or anything.

"Caden!" his father's voice shouted again. This time, there was more anger and impatience in his bark.

Cade adjusted his shorts, then pulled open his bedroom door and stepped out. He didn't bother putting on a shirt. The house was a thousand degrees, and his father had no money for air-conditioning.

"What?" Caden huffed, entering the living room and glaring at his father.

His father was in his late fifties, having got his mom pregnant in his early forties. That was the thing about men; they could continue spreading their seed well into their later years.

His mom had been some waitress who boned his father one drunken night when they were all partying. Nine months later, she popped Caden out, then took off with some dude she met at a rest stop. His mother didn't have high standards, considering she fucked his father—a man with zero manners and a raging drug problem.

Although, Caden had to give it to his father. Even though the man was a piece of shit, he still took care of Caden, raised him, and even managed to put a roof over their head. How he managed that? Caden would never know.

"Where the fuck were you?" his father asked, using a credit card to separate his coke in nice even lines.

For a man who was high three-quarters of the time, he didn't seem to have a problem separating his next hit.

"I was in my room studying," Caden answered, growing annoyed with his father's constant pestering.

"Still? Why the fuck are you reading that shit? The only thing you need to know is where the G-spot is and where your next hit is coming from." His father raised the tray with three even lines of coke and offered it to Caden.

Caden was fifteen. He'd tried weed and a bit of coke with some of his friends but still felt awkward getting high with his father.

Caden shook his head.

His father's disapproving eyes said it all. He wasn't tough enough when it came to being a man.

"You know, all that studyin' and stayin' sober and shit is gonna give the guys the wrong impression," his father said, placing the tray down and rolling up a dollar bill. "People are gonna start thinking you're some kind of homo and pansy and won't respect you like they should."

Caden had heard his father's bullshit his whole life. He believed that men should be men. They should be tough, controlling, and never show emotions. Emotions were like feelings, and only women showed their feelings.

Living in Baton, it wasn't exactly the nicest of places. They had one biker gang that called the shots and a town full of people who liked to drink and party.

"Studying is not going to make me a homo," Caden responded, getting annoyed once again. "Did you need something? Or just like pissing me off?"

His father took a hit off the tray and leaned back on the sofa as he waited for the drugs to kick in.

"Get me another glass of whiskey," he ordered, nodding toward his empty on the table.

Shaking his head, Caden grabbed the glass and was about to head to the kitchen when there was a knock at the door.

Changing his direction, he headed to the door and opened it without checking who it was. Considering the time, he figured it was probably one of his father's tricks stopping by to make a quick twenty by sucking his father's dick.

"Sheriff?" Cade asked, caught off guard by the two uniformed officers standing in the doorway. "Can I help you?"

Sheriff Burke looked past Cade and shook his head when he spotted his father.

"We're here for your pops." The sheriff nodded to his deputy, who entered the house when Caden stepped aside.

"Edgar Flanagan, you're under arrest for assault and robbery," the deputy said, stepping around the table and pulling his handcuffs off his belt. He glanced down at the tray of neatly separated drugs before shaking his head and helping his father to his feet.

"What? You got the wrong guy," his father argued, barely fighting back against the deputy. "That man had a mouth on him, and he said I could have his wallet and watch." His father glanced over at Caden before adding, "Make sure they don't steal any of my stash."

Like having his drugs confiscated was his father's greatest problem.

"Dad." Caden wasn't sure what to do. Was he supposed to go to the jail with his father? Call a lawyer? It's not like they had any money for one, anyway.

"Cade, come with me, and I'll drop you off at Mrs.

Warden's house for the night. She said you could stay with her until we get this whole mess with your father sorted."

Reluctantly, Caden followed the sheriff and his father out to the police car. He had never ridden in one before, and he wasn't sure how he felt about getting into one now.

"Hey, at least we'll be together," his father slurred as the deputy helped him into the car.

"Yeah, sure." Caden slid in next to his father and watched as a few of their neighbors came out to watch.

It wasn't long after his father went to jail that he got into a fight with another inmate and was stabbed to death by a home-made blade. It was his father's hot temper that ended up being the end of him.

Caden remained with Mrs. Warden until he turned eighteen. After that, he got his own place and started working with Marcus and the Shadow Vipers.

6

CADEN

*I*t had been about a week since the "incident." Caden hadn't spoken much to Lucas. He'd been actively trying to avoid the guy for fear that he might have another reaction or inappropriate thought involving him and rubbing his face all over the boy's body.

Not that he wanted to be creepy and make love to the guy's skin, more like he was curious as to how his soft skin might feel... rubbing up against his...

Was it soft? Would Cade's body feel coarse against his skin? Would Lucas tremble when Caden ran his fingers slowly down the smooth curve of his back?

He wasn't sure what it all meant.

When Cade was with women, he often enjoyed lying with them and caressing their soft skin after fucking their brains out.

Yes, he fucked them rough and hard and loved the way they cried out his name just before they came. But once it was all over, he liked to hold them close to his chest and feel their tender skin up against his body.

Something about their silky, smooth skin and the beating of their heart calmed him and took him to a place where he could be at peace. That peaceful feeling never lasted long, but for those first fifteen minutes or so, he felt like all his troubles had faded.

Cade never mentioned this to any of the guys in the crew. Showing tenderness or anything that resembled romance was looked down upon. Guys in the gang were supposed to be tough. They didn't discuss feelings or emotions or how much they enjoyed a good cuddle after an intense boning session.

That all remained unspoken.

These new thoughts were his to unpack and figure out all on his own.

Whatever. He didn't need anyone's help.

"Hey, Alexis, how's it going?" Caden asked, taking a seat on one of the barstools.

"Hey, Cade. Not much. I'm low-key freaking out here."

"What? Why?"

"My dance instructor had to cancel on me. Apparently, her mother fell sick, so she's off to Texas to go and be with her."

"And... you're upset that she's seeing her sick mother? That sounds mean, even for you." Cade gave a chuckle, knowing it had to be more than just that. Alexis was tough, but she wasn't evil.

The blonde-and-pink bombshell gave Cade the middle finger.

"It was for my wedding. I hired a professional to teach me how to dance. Then I thought I could do a little performance at the ceremony for Jake. You know, show him how much I love him."

Alexis and Jake had recently gotten engaged, and half the town was invited to their wedding. It was in a couple of months, and Caden was still trying to find a way to avoid attending.

Stomach flu? Leprosy? Cat stuck in a tree?

He knew he was being a jerk, and there was no way in hell Marcus would allow him to miss young Alexis's nuptials. While they might not be related, everyone in the gang was treated as family. So, when one of them got married, they all happily attended—even if deep down, the thought of watching two people profess their love to one another made him want to take a drill to his eyes.

"Can't you hire someone else?" Caden asked, wondering why this was such a big deal. There must be loads of people around who know how to slow dance or do the chicken... whatever it's called.

He didn't care much for dancing. Shaking his hips and getting his nut sack all sweaty didn't exactly sound like a good time.

Alexis shook her head. "I've tried that, but everyone local is already booked or can't make it."

"I could do it," a voice beside Cade offered.

They both looked up to see Lucas standing next to Cade with a tray full of empty glasses.

He placed the tray down on the bar and slid in between Caden and the barstool next to him.

"What sort of dance do you need to learn?"

"Anything. I'm not much of a dancer when there's no pole in front of me." Lucas and Caden exchanged a look. "Oh! You know what would be cool? Learning that fancy dance named after Walt Disney."

"Walt Disney?" Lucas asked, looking confused as hell. "Oh! Do you mean the waltz?"

"Yeah! That's the one. Do you know that dance, Luc?" Alexis's eyes lit up at the possibility that she might have found her new dance instructor.

"Well, yeah, I know how to waltz. But for that, I would suggest that I teach both you and your fiancé. Then, at least, you can both dance together," Lucas suggested.

"Were you a dance teacher or something?" Alexis asked, leaning up against the bar and showing the guys why her husband was really marrying her.

Her tits were two sizes too big for her body. There was no chance in hell that they were natural, but that didn't matter to her fiancé, Jake. He loved boobs and took every opportunity to remind people that he did.

"Umm, no. I studied musical theater in college."

"Oh my god! That's amazing! Did you do any musicals or plays? I love seeing musicals," Alexis gushed.

One would never guess, given the large number of tattoos that stained her body.

Alexis was a blend of Pamela Anderson from *Baywatch* and Katey Sagal, who played Gemma in *Sons of Anarchy*. Little did people realize that she was also a closeted Broadway diva—*apparently*.

Lucas's face flushed. He glanced around the bar as if worried that someone might have overheard them.

Was he embarrassed?

Caden was still having trouble trying to read the boy's body language.

"I did a few shows in college and had a few auditions before—" His voice caught in his throat. A pained look flashed across his face. Clearly, this was something that he was not comfortable discussing. "Well, anyway, whatever dances you want to learn, I can teach you."

Lucas picked up the tray and walked around the bar to where the dishwasher was tucked away. He opened the latch and began loading the dirty glasses.

"Ah! I'm so excited! You're the best." Alexis pulled out her cell and unlocked it. "Give me your number, and I'll set something up."

Lucas's body tensed. He remained bent over for a moment before slowly straightening up.

"Umm, actually, I don't have a cell phone."

"What?" Alexis looked shocked, like her best friend had just told her that the sky was actually a deep shade of orange instead of a gentle, soft blue. "How do you not have a cell phone? Can people actually function without one?" Then her eyes widened. "*Oh*, is it some kind of weird religious thing or something?"

It was clear that Alexis had trouble fathoming that someone could actually survive not being a slave to their phone.

Alexis's social media feed read like an audition for *Biker Chicks Gone Wild*. There wasn't a thing that she and Jake did that didn't end up on that damn thing. Caden was surprised that they hadn't started an *OnlyFans* page, given some of the pretty raunchy videos that they sometimes posted.

Caden had to admit that he had popped a boner a time or two while scrolling through her page. Seeing her and Jake in that hot tub video they had posted had made his jeans painfully tight.

"Umm, no. I just... don't have one." The boy's face was beet red as he continued to stack the washer with mugs and pint glasses.

Caden had never met a person who didn't own a cell phone. Well, perhaps his grandparents when he was younger. But that was before cell phones became an extension of people's bodies.

Alexis was right. How did the boy function without a cell phone? How did he pay his bills? Post on social media? Watch porn?

What self-respecting guy in their twenties didn't beat his meat to porn on his cell phone?

FYI, don't ever pick up a guy's cell phone. You don't want to know what microbes or bodily fluids are caked onto that thing.

You've. Been. Warned.

"So, how will I get ahold of you?" Alexis asked, still not convinced that Lucas was telling the truth.

"How about we meet up tomorrow around eleven? This will give us a few hours to practice before our shift starts at night. You got a place where we can practice?"

Alexis nodded and then wrote down her home address on a bar napkin. "We've got a large garage that we can practice in and a portable stereo that can play music."

"That sounds perfect," Lucas said, glancing up at Cade before blushing and glancing away just as quickly. "Got to run," he muttered before dashing back around the bar and disappearing into the back once more.

Caden was confused. Something didn't feel right about the elusive Lucas Braden.

He spotted Marcus sitting in a booth toward the back of the bar, scrolling through his cell phone, and decided that he should probably go and have a chat with his boss.

"Hey, boss, got a sec?"

Marcus placed his phone down on the table and nodded. "Sure, what's up?"

Caden slid onto the bench across from him and did a quick scan of the bar to make sure that no one was in earshot of their conversation.

"I was just wondering about Luc. What do you know about the guy?"

"What do you mean?" Marcus asked, confusion and concern growing on his face.

"Well, where did he move from? What did he do for work before moving here? The guy always changes the subject whenever you ask him anything personal. Did you know that the dude doesn't even have a cell phone?"

Marcus glanced over at where Lucas was wiping down a table and wiping sweat off his forehead.

"Why? Has he done something that I should be concerned about? Has he done anything inappropriate?"

Caden's brows furrowed as he shook his head.

"No, not that I'm aware of. I'm just saying there's something off about the kid. There's something that he's hiding. I can feel it."

If the boy was dangerous, Caden needed to protect his family. All the guys in the gang were under his protection. Even his massive six-foot-four beast of a boss.

Marcus's jaw tightened. He interlocked his fingers, then leaned forward on the table.

"Look around this bar. Everyone in this place has secrets—things that we don't want the world to know about. Our lusts, our desires, our demons, even our pasts. We all carry our own baggage. Some may weigh heavier than others. But ultimately, it is our baggage to carry. All of us are entitled to our secrets—to decide when and with whom we will share those secrets. Is Lucas not entitled to his secrets? His own story to protect and keep hidden if he so chooses?"

His boss was right. Caden was no saint. He'd done his fair share of activities that would have landed him in jail or earned him a first-class ticket to that eternal after-party buried deep beneath the earth's core.

"Not having a cell phone, while uncommon, may be due

to legitimate reasons. You're probably also wondering what someone like Lucas is doing working in a place like this?"

Caden nodded. He was dying to ask his boss but didn't want to question his decisions. Marcus might be a nice guy, but he also had a temper that you didn't want directed at you.

"One of the first questions Lucas asked me when he walked into the bar was about our hiring process—specifically, whether we conduct background checks or call for references."

Caden's head snapped in the direction of the young man, who was now busy tucking in chairs that patrons seemed to leave anywhere they liked. Caden once found a chair sitting outside the women's washroom. Did women stand guard while they peed?

"See? So he is a criminal!" Caden declared triumphantly. He wasn't crazy, after all.

Marcus shook his head in disappointment.

"What are some of the reasons that someone might not want a background check conducted on them?"

Caden thought about the question for a moment. He wasn't really sure.

"Because they might be on the run? Or hiding from someone they don't want to find them?" Caden asked, staring at the elusive young man who looked like the last person who would ever commit a crime or be on the run from the police.

"Exactly. It's hard to find places of employment these days that don't run background and credit checks. Even setting up a cell-phone plan requires a credit check," Marcus explained.

Caden turned his attention back to his boss. "Do you think that Luc might be in some kind of danger?" Caden asked, suddenly ashamed that he assumed the worst about the shy boy who got nervous around burly, tattooed men.

"Not sure. That's one of the reasons that I hired him." Caden looked at Marcus, confused. "It wasn't for his mad skills at washing dishes. The boy was clearly lying through his teeth during the job interview. But at least if I gave him a job, I could watch out for him and, if the time ever came, offer the kid protection or assistance if needed."

"Now I feel like an idiot for assuming the worst."

Marcus reached across the table and grabbed hold of Cade's shoulder.

"It's because you care about this crew and your family." He gave Caden a warm smile and released his shoulder. "Now, I want you to keep what we discussed just between you and me. Lucas's past is his own to share with us when he's ready. For the time being, all we can do is watch out for him and be that supportive ear if he ever wants to reach out."

This was why everyone loved Marcus. He looked out for everyone and never forced anyone to do something they weren't ready to do.

"Now, don't you have something to do? I'm not paying you to sit here and keep me company. I've got online porn for that."

Cade rolled his eyes.

"Are you even able to get it up at your ripe old age?"

Marcus's eyes narrowed.

It was time for Cade to leave. *Quick.*

Not wasting any time, Cade slid out of the booth and jogged over to the front of the bar. In a few hours, patrons would be stopping by for their after-work drinks.

The sound of pebbles crunching beneath his feet made Caden cringe with every step he took. If he wanted this to work, he needed to remain undetected.

Throughout the night, he watched Lucas from a distance.

At first glance, the boy appeared to be just like any other hardworking American. He cleared off tables, wiped up spilled alcohol, and helped Alexis change out beer kegs.

Everything seemed to fit the role of busboy.

But when Caden took a step back and decided to look a little deeper, he started to notice the subtle red flags.

The flinches every time a large man jostled him, the lack of eye contact, the smiles that quickly vanished when he thought that no one was looking.

Whatever it was that drove Lucas from his previous life must have been big.

Caden needed to know.

Not that he was worried for the safety of his friends and family, but because he needed to know what he was protecting Lucas from. Yes, he had made the decision that

Lucas was now a part of his family, and if he was in trouble, he was under Caden's protection.

All through the night, Caden ran through scenarios in his head: an abusive father, trouble with a violent street gang, perhaps gambling debts that had gotten out of control.

Whatever it was, Caden needed to protect the boy from the threat.

And at what cost? that annoying voice inside his head asked.

I'll do whatever is necessary.

He heard the voice inside his head begin to chuckle.

They have a word for what you are doing... it's called stalking.

No. He wasn't stalking. A stalker was a creepy dude who followed people home late at night and peeked in their windows...

And what is it that you think that you are doing? that pesky voice asked him once again.

Fuck you.

He watched as Lucas cut across Old Man Benson's field and headed toward the barn he had out back.

What was Lucas doing?

Pulling open the barn door, Lucas disappeared into the wooden structure.

He ignored that feeling in the pit of his stomach that told him he had crossed so many lines—starting with following Lucas home after work to now, about to peek through his open barn windows.

No, he was not a stalker. Or a peeping Tom.

Try telling that to the judge as he passes his sentence at your serial killer murder trial.

Seriously, what was wrong with him?

Crouching down next to one of the back windows, Caden slowly lifted his head so he could peek inside without being noticed.

Not creepy at all.

God, if the guy ever found out, he would fucking kill him.

Well, maybe not kill him because of the size difference, but probably never talk to him again.

Or slip laxatives into his beer.

Either way, Caden would be fucked.

A light flickered on inside the barn, followed by another, and then soft music began to play.

Outside, Caden watched as Lucas climbed the wooden ladder up to the loft, which appeared to open up to a large living space.

It was the end of June, so the temperature outside at night was warm and comforting. Come wintertime, though, the barn's temperature would not be so welcoming.

He wondered how long Lucas planned to live here. It couldn't be comfortable or even enjoyable to reside in a large wooden structure that had previously housed animals and stored hay.

From what Caden could recall, Old Man Benson used to keep three horses in this barn, using them for work around the farm.

Why wouldn't Lucas just rent a normal place? There were plenty of apartments for rent scattered around town.

Because most places performed credit checks and asked for references. He doubted that Old Man Benson did either of those things. He was a cheap man who only did the bare minimum.

One by one, the lights inside the barn turned off as the new boy in town prepared for a well-deserved good night's sleep.

Another part of the Lucas mystery had been unlocked.

The more Caden uncovered, the more determined he became.

He needed to do more to help this kid. He wasn't sure why he felt so protective, but god help the person who ever attempted to take advantage of his boy or do him any harm.

Lucas Braden was under his protection now.

As the last light turned off, Caden stole one last glance up at the loft. Somewhere, hidden in all that darkness, was a scared young man with a secret he kept hidden from all.

It was getting late, and he was already tired. Plus, he had his own little princess to check in on.

7

LUCAS

*A*lexis and her fiancé were not horrible. They just lacked finesse, coordination, and, of course, the ability to let go and feel the music. Jake had a bit of trouble putting his manhood aside and becoming one with the music. Alexis... well, she was a little too comfortable letting the music take control.

Lucas had to keep reminding Alexis that children would most likely be in attendance at their wedding, so it was probably best if she kept her vag off Jake's bulging hard-on.

Like, seriously. The two acted like a pair of horny college students alone in a cabin in the dead of summer. At first, Lucas thought that perhaps they were playing with him, trying to make him uncomfortable with their borderline pornographic dance or porn-star mating ritual... whatever one might call it.

It was Lucas's fault, really. He asked them if there were any dances they were familiar with, to which Alexis pulled out a chair, shoved Jake into the seat, and then proceeded to give the man a million-dollar lap dance.

Nope. Not wedding-appropriate.

Definitely not.

Alexis failed to mention that she used to work as a stripper and that Jake was her number one client. She stopped stripping once they started dating.

Talk about a *meet-cute* romance. Eat that, Hallmark!

"You guys are doing great. Let's try that again, one more time."

"I don't see why I wouldn't just have my hands on her hips in the first place. That way, I can grind my junk against her and remind her why she's marrying me."

Jake was a bit of a pig. He fit that rough-and-tough biker stereotype that was often seen in the movies or on cop reality shows. In a way, it was kind of hot, but also, it was kind of annoying. *We get it; you've got a big dick.* And if anyone was the lucky one in this scenario, it was Jake. He was getting to marry one of the sweetest girls Lucas had ever met.

Yes, she looked rough on the outside, but she also possessed class and charm that she tried to keep hidden from the rest of the guys. Lucas sensed that she believed it wasn't acceptable to show such a soft side. Yet here she was, learning to waltz with her fiancé, hoping to class up her wedding, which was sure to be overrun by loud men with big egos and mouths just as dirty as her man's.

"Jake!" Alexis shouted as she slapped her fiancé's shoulder. "Stop being so rude. Plus, we all know the real reason you are marrying me is because of these." Alexis shook her chest, smiling as her man's eyes went wide and his lips parted in a hungry grin.

If anyone has ever wondered what a starving lion looks like when it comes across an injured deer, it kind of resembled Jake's current expression—except less man-boner and more salivation.

They really were perfect for each other.

"Okay, let's try it one more time."

Lucas pressed play on Alexis's laptop—the source of their waltz music, thanks to the magic of YouTube.

He watched as his students began to move together. With enough practice, their movements would eventually become a dance. For now, at least it didn't look like Jake was trying to impregnate his fiancée on their pretend dance floor.

"Wow, who knew that Jake had moves?" a deep voice asked, startling the trio mid-waltz.

Lucas looked up just as Caden stepped into the garage.

The man was created by the sex gods.

He was wearing a torn, sleeveless Rob Zombie T-shirt and tight blue jeans that were ripped across his thick thighs. To say that the material barely stretched across his legs was an understatement. Caden definitely did not skip leg days.

For a straight man, Caden sure knew how to dress. His clothing was stylish yet masculine, current but looked like it had been used and worn. Not to mention that every article of clothing hugged the man in all the right places.

"I've got moves that will put all you guys to shame," Jake bragged, grinding his junk deep against his lady.

The move was clearly something that man had seen once

—or twice—in a pornographic film. Probably starring some big-breasted woman and a dirty, slow-speaking mechanic. Lucas was getting the sense that that was the sort of thing Jake was into—big boobs and blue-collar men.

"Argh!" Alexis protested, breaking away from her fiancé and taking a step back. "I felt the head and everything!"

Jake chuckled. "That was the whole point, babe."

"Have you been hard this entire time?" Alexis shouted, not seeming to care which of her neighbors might overhear.

Jake nodded like the horny pig that he was.

"God, I have no idea why I love you," she said, clearly not upset about the whole dancing while hard incident. "So what are you doing here?" Alexis asked, turning her attention back to their newest guest.

Cade held up a tray of coffees.

"Thought you all might like a cup."

"Fuck yes," Jake cheered, jumping around Alexis and pulling a cup loose from the tray.

That was awfully kind of Caden.

Lucas didn't realize that the three of them were the "bring each other a coffee out of the blue" kind of close.

Cade passed a cup to Alexis and then walked over to where Lucas was standing.

"I wasn't sure how you take your coffee, so I grabbed some cream and sugar on the side." He passed the tray, pulling a cup free for himself.

"Wow, that was really nice of you," Lucas acknowledged.

He wasn't sure how a straight man would react if he said that it was a sweet gesture. Knowing his luck, the man would punch him in the face, then resume drinking his coffee. So, to be safe, he decided to keep his response as generic as possible.

"Nah, it was nothing. I was out grabbing a cup and thought I would see how the lessons were going."

"Don't you live on the other side of town?" Jake asked, lifting his lid and taking a sip.

Caden's lips parted, appearing annoyed that he had been called out on his actions. "I like to walk, asshole."

Lucas tried not to smile. It was really sweet that Cade had gone out of his way to bring them all a coffee.

What are you doing? Don't go falling in love with some sexy-ass straight boy when all he's done is buy you a coffee. Did you not learn anything?

Lucas hated that voice of reason inside his head. The bastard had taken up residence ever since he'd met his ex. He liked to remind Lucas when he was being dumb and idiotic.

The jerk was right. He needed to calm down and not make this into more than what it was.

A coffee.

That's it.

Nothing more.

"So, how are they doing?" Caden asked, lowering his voice as if trying to prevent the neighbors from hearing.

"Nailed it. Ready for *Dancing with the Stars* and shit," Jake responded with that over-confident tone Lucas was starting to recognize as his default setting.

"Actually, they're doing really well. Alexis has such grace that she can move her body into positions few are able to. And Jake? Well, he's got the ego of a rock star."

"And a dick to match," Jake added.

Another slap against Jake's chest. This one made Lucas chuckle.

"He's actually a really good teacher," Alexis noted, taking a step toward them and giving Lucas one of her warmest smiles. She really was a pretty woman.

Lucas could feel his cheeks flushing. He really missed dancing and singing, and teaching Alexis and her fiancé had reminded him just how much.

"Want to see what we learned?" Alexis asked.

"For sure," Caden answered, taking a step aside and positioning himself in a viewer's stance.

Alexis set both of their coffees on the floor and wrapped her arms around her man. Then she paused. She glanced over at Caden and Lucas, giving them both a questioning look.

"How about you two join us? This way, we can see how Lucas really moves on a dance floor."

"What? You mean, like, me and Lucas dance... *together*?"

Caden sounded shocked at the suggestion.

Wow, the boy really was straight as an arrow. He could almost hear Caden's butt cheeks slam closed. *Hate to tell you, precious, but in our situation, it would be me getting my butt assaulted.*

Lucas rolled his eyes. He got it. Some guys weren't comfortable dancing with other dudes, but still, the way Caden had reacted kind of hurt his feelings.

"Yeah. What? Are you too afraid to get close to a man and dance with him for a few minutes? Come on! I need to see how Lucas does it," Alexis protested.

Lucas didn't like people feeling pressured into doing something they weren't comfortable with. He was bullied enough growing up; he didn't need others to be bullied as well.

"Don't worry about it, Alexis. I can dance the part alone," Lucas offered.

"Well, no. It's... fine." Caden appeared conflicted, like he wasn't sure what he should be doing. His body shifted from side to side, and his eyes kept darting from person to person. "I don't mind. Really."

Caden's soft blue eyes flicked to Lucas, searching momentarily for confirmation or guidance as to how their little dance should go.

"Really, it's not necessary. I can show them on my own," Lucas offered one more time. In college, they rehearsed without partners all the time. While the dance may not look the prettiest, it served its purpose and got the job done.

Shaking his head, Caden grabbed both of their coffees and set them on the floor out of the way.

"It's no big deal. Just two dudes dancing together in a garage," Caden said, placing both of his hands on Lucas's hips.

Clearly, Caden had never waltzed before either.

Lucas smiled.

"Fine." He started the music again on the laptop and quickly explained the steps to Caden.

Placing Caden's hands in the appropriate positions, Lucas took a deep breath and then began to move to the music.

It was hard to concentrate. Holding on to Caden's hand with one and holding his muscular shoulder with the other. Not to mention staring into the sex god's smoldering blue eyes.

Talk about intimate.

How was it possible for one man to be so freakin' good-looking? His eyes were a captivating aqua-blue that resembled the beaches in Fiji—not that Lucas had ever been. And Cade's sexy beard added a sense of roughness that made Lucas's dick extremely hard.

Then there were the bulging muscles. It was clear that the man spent hours in the gym daily, perfecting every curve and indent in his gorgeous, manly body. Gay men and women everywhere thanked him.

Having Caden's body only a few inches from his was torture. It was like holding a chilled glass of water in front of a man who had been wandering the desert for two weeks and not allowing him to drink. The pain was excruciating.

Ouch!

That... was real pain.

"Shit! Sorry!" Cade blurted, horrified after stepping on Lucas's toes for the third consecutive time in a row.

Lucas couldn't help but smile. He would gladly take any form of physical contact from Caden—even the kind that brought physical pain and discomfort to his body.

Pain and discomfort. Now his ass was taking notice.

"You're doing great. Just focus on my eyes and let my body guide you." He didn't have the heart to tell Cade that he was a horrible dancer. It had taken all of Cade's courage to dance with another man, so Lucas was going to do everything he could to boost the man's ego.

"Don't worry if you can't get it, dude," Jake said next to them. "Dudes weren't meant to dance together, so that's why you aren't in step with each other."

Lucas was getting tired of Jake's homophobic comments and piggish ways. He was getting close to ending this lesson.

"There's nothing wrong with two dudes dancing. Actually, I find it quite hot watching two guys together. If you don't smarten up, Jake, I'm going to go join Cade and Luc in the middle of their hot man-sandwich," Alexis scolded.

Lucas got the sense that Alexis was a little adventurous when it came to sex. If she hadn't already, it was only a matter of time before she convinced Jake to let her peg him. For a petite girl, she could be a total powerhouse.

"Do you hear that, Luc? Alexis is up for a little three-way with you and me. Now all we have to do is send Jake out for a pack of smokes," Caden noted, giving them all an evil grin.

Could he ever sleep with a girl just to get naked with Cade? No. Definitely not. He was a three-star gay and planned on remaining that way. He had never fucked a girl, kissed a girl, and was born via C-section.

"As flattering as that sounds, I'm not really one for sharing," Lucas answered.

Caden's lips turned up in a mischievous smirk.

Was he... pleased?

Caden turned toward Alexis as he stumbled over Lucas's feet. "Sorry, but it sounds like you'll have to continue being disappointed with Jake's lovemaking skills."

Jake flipped them both the finger.

The music continued as Lucas gave instructions to the couple and continued to encourage Cade with his movements.

It was strange. Never in a million years would Lucas have imagined that he would be dancing with any of the guys he worked with at the bar, least of all the hot-as-fuck bouncer with dangerously smooth hips and deliciously kissable lips.

And the way that Cade kept his eyes locked with his...

Fuck. And those strong hands gripping his body...

Eyes still locked with his partner, Lucas concentrated on not popping a boner or leaning forward and kissing the man. He was pretty sure that was instant grounds for death.

For a straight man, Caden seemed pretty comfortable being so close and intimate with Lucas. In the beginning, his body was tense, and his heartbeat was racing, but as time passed by, Caden seemed to relax and become more comfortable with having a man as a dance partner.

Lucas had to admit, the past few weeks, he had been nervous as shit around the hunky tattooed beefcake, partly because he was turned-on as fuck, and partly because he was afraid to get close to another alpha male.

His ex was an alpha. It was one of the things that turned him on so much.

He knew that Cade was straight but still worried about how he might be treated. Alpha straight men didn't exactly have the best track record when it came to drooling gay men.

But seeing Cade today and seeing the generous kindness

he was showing his friends, Lucas was starting to feel more comfortable around the tatted biker.

Now, if he could just get his dick to obey and not threaten to stab Caden in the thigh, they might have a chance at being friends.

"Shit! Is that the time?" Alexis cried out, staring at the small digital clock that sat on one of the shelves. "We got to go meet Mom and Dad for lunch in an hour."

Disappointed, Lucas pulled away from Cade and tried to act normal. He was already missing the feeling of having Caden's hand in his and their bodies only inches apart.

The man even smelled great, like Irish Spring soap and leather.

"Thanks again for the lessons, Luc. Think we can meet again later in the week?"

"For sure," Lucas answered, turning off the music and trying not to gaze longingly over at Caden.

"How about I walk you home?" Caden offered, startling Lucas and giving him a mini-panic attack.

Heat rushed through Lucas's cheeks. There was no way he wanted Caden to walk him home and discover that he was living in a barn! How embarrassing.

"Umm, actually, it's alright. I have a few errands to run before work tonight, but thanks for offering."

Alexis and Jake disappeared into the house while Caden followed Lucas out onto the sidewalk.

"It's okay. I really don't mind joining you."

"No. Don't worry about it. I've got a lot to do and don't want to drag you around with me."

He would have loved to spend more time with Cade, but he didn't want him to see where he lived, and he didn't have extra cash to spend pretending to buy shit he didn't need.

As if sensing his trepidation, Caden finally gave up and relented.

"Fine. In that case, here," Caden said, stopping for a moment and reaching into his back pocket. He pulled out a small cell phone and passed it over to Lucas. "I got you this."

Lucas stared down at the cell in Caden's hand and wondered what the heck was going on.

"I know you don't have a cell, so I figured you could use this. Don't worry. It's new, and it's a burner phone, just in case you're worried about people tracking your movements or the government spying on you." Caden let out a soft chuckle.

He stared at Cade for a moment, unsure of how to react. He needed a cell phone, and the gesture was both kind and extremely moving, but he didn't want to have to explain to Cade why he couldn't buy a cell phone on his own. The truth was both embarrassing and degrading.

"I... ah..." Still no words came to him.

His heart pounded in his chest as he fought the urge to leap into the man's arms and hug him... and also run away.

"Here," Cade said, placing the phone into the palm of his hand. "I loaded it up with three hundred dollars' worth of minutes, so that should last you a bit of time. I also programmed my number into your cell so you can text me if you need anything."

Lucas stared at him with such confusion. There was a flurry of emotions currently coursing through his body.

Why was this guy, he barely knew, being so damn nice to him?

Should he accept the gift?

Would Caden take offense if he didn't?

Why would this man, who owed him nothing, do such an incredibly kind thing for him?

He wasn't used to people being so nice.

In Los Angeles, people tended to prioritize their own self-interests. They perceived each interaction as a chance to enhance their image and fulfill their own personal desires.

People didn't just buy you coffees and cell phones without ulterior motives.

But what possible ulterior motive could Caden have?

Lucas wasn't rich; he didn't own anything. He didn't even have a goddamn credit card! He had to stop using his cards the night he left his ex. He'd withdrawn the three grand he'd saved up over the years, so he at least had money to live off until he found a job and could get back on his feet. Paying in cash was always the safest bet.

Thinking of all this, Lucas was reminded just how fucked-up his life really was. The realization made him feel even more depressed.

"I... really can't accept this," he finally said, staring at the cell and trying not to tear up.

Lucas felt two fingers graze the underside of his chin and gently lift his face upward.

"You can, and you will. At the bar, we're a family. We

help each other out. I don't know much about you or where you came from, but I do recognize when someone is going through some shit. So this is my way of helping to make things just a bit easier for you."

Lucas felt his eyes begin to water. He truly appreciated the help and couldn't believe that someone he hardly knew was willing to help him out.

"There are no strings attached, no judgment. Just one friend helping out another."

Caden's words meant the world to him. Knowing that someone cared enough to want to help gave him hope—hope that he might one day see a better future.

"Thank you, Cade. I really appreciate this," Lucas said, holding up the cell phone.

"It's no big deal."

But it was. A big fuckin' deal.

"Catch you later, kid," Caden added, giving him one of his panty-dropping smiles.

Lucas felt his heart swoon as he watched his sexy knight in shining armor strut away.

He was in such big trouble.

Flipping open his new phone, Lucas opened the contacts folder. And there, standing all by its lonesome, were two little words, "Sexy-ass Bouncer."

Smiling, he selected the name and shot off a text.

Lucas: Who Dis?

He watched as Caden pulled his cell phone out of his

pocket and slowed. Stopping, he turned and shot Lucas one of the sexist smirks he had ever seen.

Caden typed out a message quickly before shoving his phone back in his pocket.

Lucas's phone dinged.

> Sexy-ass Bouncer: I thought the name said it all.

Shaking his head, Lucas turned and began walking in the opposite direction.

Why were all the charming guys he liked always straight?

8

___

CADEN

*D*ancing with Luc had been the hardest thing Caden had ever done. Literally the hardest! It took all of his willpower and concentration not to pop a boner while dancing with the guy. The smell of the boy's lotion, the feel of his body as it bumped against his, the terrified yet hungry look in his eyes. All of it. It was all torture!

It took every last ounce of his straight-bro control not to throw the guy down on the bench, rip his pants down around his ankles, and shove his fucking cock deep inside those perky ass cheeks of his. The hunger he felt was like nothing he had ever experienced before.

What the fuck was happening to him?

He had never felt this way before, not even with a woman. Sex had always just been sex—a fun activity he enjoyed and that made him feel good.

But this? This was something else entirely. And to be honest, it kind of scared him.

Caden had been raised in a hypermasculine environment. He'd been raised to believe that guys needed to be guys. They didn't show emotions, didn't talk about their feelings, and definitely did not fantasize about throwing down their male coworkers and pounding the shit out of them.

His thoughts were both confusing and foreign. In all his life, he had never once felt sexually attracted to another dude. Was that even an option?

What was it about Lucas that had him feeling all these strange feelings?

Was it possible to want to devour somebody yet serve and protect them all at the same time?

There was something about the boy that was getting under his skin. Some carnal need. An awakening he had never experienced before. He wasn't sure what it was, but it both terrified and excited him.

Standing in a towel, Caden stared at the three-inch scar just below his left rib cage. The scar had faded over the years but was a constant reminder of how close he had come to having his life cut short. He hadn't noticed the man sneak up behind him in the shower. Thankfully, his cellmate, Dre, had been showering two showers over from him and jumped in before his attacker had an opportunity to do lethal damage.

DeSantis, his attacker, belonged to a rival crew that dealt drugs out of Austin, Texas. He had been instructed to send Marcus a message to keep off their territory by eliminating one of Marcus's crew members. And who better to target than the vulnerable, naked man showering with his eyes closed?

Caden wasn't even aware that he had been stabbed until DeSantis's face smashed up against the tile wall, and his home-made blade had fallen to the floor.

Pain shot through Caden's side as he reached down to inspect the open wound that was leaking blood at an alarming rate.

Shouts and grunts ensued as Dre pummeled DeSantis into the tiled shower floor.

Caden watched, confused and in pain, as Dre continued to beat the man to a bloody pulp. After what felt like an eternity, two guards rushed in and pulled Dre off DeSantis.

Bleeding and feeling lightheaded, Caden collapsed against the shower wall and watched as the guards pulled a snarling Dre out of the shower just moments before a third guard rushed in to tend to Caden and his wounds.

Caden spent the next three days in the infirmary attempting to avoid infection. His assassin's blade wasn't exactly the most sanitary of objects.

When he was finally permitted to return to his cell, he discovered that Dre had been moved to another wing of the prison, and his would-be assassin had been placed in solitary for a week. No further attempts had been made on his life during the rest of his two-year stay in prison.

Trailing his fingers along his scar, he wondered what Marcus and the guys would think if they discovered the confusing thoughts he was having about their latest brother. Would they view it as reprehensible? An act of betrayal? Would they treat him differently?

Marcus had never given him a reason to suspect that he

would treat anyone differently based on whom they chose to sleep with. In fact, Marcus went out of his way to show him and the other guys from the crew just how much he appreciated them.

Caden had just turned twenty-four when he took the fall for Marcus and his brothers. They had been transporting cocaine and heroin over state lines when the police flagged down their van. Knowing they had been caught, Caden insisted that Marcus and Ace slip out of the van as they were driving across a bridge before he pulled over and allowed the police to search their vehicle.

At first, Marcus had protested, insisting that he was their leader and he would never abandon his crew. But Caden pushed back, arguing that he was part of the family and family protected one another. While Marcus might be the leader, he also had other responsibilities that he needed to tend to. Caden would take the hit for the crew and, in time, rejoin them as a free man.

Luckily, a judge took pity on Cade and only sentenced him to two years in prison, removing the heroin charge—something to do with issues of chain of custody while processing the heroin into evidence.

During the next two years, Marcus and rotating members of the crew stopped by to visit Cade. They added money to his commissary and even smuggled in a few items of pleasure—one of them being a pocket pussy for those long and lonely nights while his roommate was sleeping.

Caden had laughed his ass off when he saw the silicone pussy. The guys really were the best.

"I'll never forget what you did for Ace and me," Marcus said to Cade once during his weekly visits.

While Marcus wanted to do the right thing for his crew, he also wanted to protect his stepbrother, Ace. The thought of Ace being sent to prison, where Marcus couldn't protect him, was something that Cade knew weighed heavily on the man. It was one of the reasons he pushed so hard when Marcus tried to remain in the vehicle with him when they were about to be pulled over. Caden knew the struggle his boss was facing and decided to remove the decision from his hands.

Taking a breath, Caden ran his hand across the condensation that had accumulated on the bathroom mirror. They had all been through a lot of shit together as a crew, and no matter what, they always had each other's backs.

He hoped that, no matter what happened in the future, they would always continue to have his.

9

LUCAS

Taking a deep breath, Lucas knocked on the office door before he lost his courage or talked himself out of it for the thousandth time that day.

You can do this. He's a reasonable boss. Plus, it's a win-win for both of them.

Still, Marcus had been so nice to him these past few weeks that he felt guilty asking him for another favor.

What if he says no?

Then he does, and you find something else to make up the difference.

"Come in," Marcus growled from the other side of the door.

Perhaps this wasn't a good time after all.

Still holding his breath, he turned the knob and stepped into the tiny office.

"Luc. Everything okay? What can I do for you?" Marcus

asked, looking up from the file folder he had opened on his desk.

Lucas closed the door behind him, then stood awkwardly in front of his boss's desk.

He could feel his knees begin to shake.

Fuck, why was he such a chicken in front of these big, strong men?

"Umm, well. I've noticed that the bar could use a bit of cleaning."

Marcus raised an eyebrow and leaned back in his chair like he didn't like what he was hearing.

Lucas felt his palms begin to sweat, and his heart was racing a mile a minute.

Shit, this wasn't going well. Marcus looked pissed.

"The bar's not up to your standards?" Marcus asked, crossing his arms over his chest as he glared.

"No. No. That's not what I meant." Lucas suddenly felt flustered. Perhaps he should just apologize and leave the office immediately.

No. He needed to do this. He couldn't spend his whole life running.

"What I meant to say is that perhaps I could work an extra shift or two overnight to give the place a deep clean. This way, it wouldn't impact your customers, and it could help spruce up the place a little bit."

Marcus's glare softened. He didn't look like he was ready to rip off his head anymore or make kindling out of his arms and legs.

"And you're suggesting this because you think my bar is dirty?"

Lucas blushed. "Well... nooo." He paused for a moment as he tried to collect his thoughts. "To be honest, I kind of need to make a bit of extra money, so I thought this might be a good way to help us both out. But if you don't like the idea, I totally understand, and I'm sorry that I said anything. Please don't fire me."

All traces of annoyance had disappeared from his boss's face. He stood and walked around his desk, resting his butt on the corner. Marcus reached out and placed his hand on Lucas's shoulder.

"Your job is never in jeopardy here. Unless you steal or hurt someone, I won't ever fire you from this job. You're family now, and family takes care of one another."

It was nice knowing that Marcus saw him as more than just an employee. Most companies say you're family but dump you when the bottom line is threatened. Working at Ride 'em Hard and being part of Marcus's new family somehow felt right. He wasn't quite sure why, but he thought it had something to do with the closeness of its members. Who knew that a biker gang could be so sweet?

"And as for your proposal, that sounds like a great idea," Marcus said, giving Lucas a firm squeeze on his shoulder. He stood and began walking back around his desk.

"Oh! Thank you, boss! You won't regret it!" Lucas cheered, suddenly feeling like a huge weight had been lifted off his chest. If he could make just a few extra dollars a week, that would help him save and get out of that shithole barn ASAP.

Feeling excited and hopeful, he jumped to his feet and rushed to the door before his boss had a chance to change his mind.

"Oh, since you'll be working overnight, I'll double your pay rate since we need to include 'danger pay.'"

"Danger pay?" Lucas asked, looking over his shoulder. Suddenly, he wasn't so sure that working alone overnight was such a good idea.

Marcus chuckled. "Relax, it's just what they call it. Basically, you get extra money because you're working alone and everything is closed. Oh, that reminds me. Since everything will be closed while you work, you'll need to bring your own food for your break. I'll give you an extra fifty dollars per night on top of your regular pay to cover the added food costs."

So, double his usual pay, plus an extra fifty dollars a night? Holy shit! That was definitely going to help him with expenses and perhaps even help him begin saving up some money.

With excitement coursing through his veins, he turned and ran back to his boss's desk.

"Thank you, thank you! You're going to be so impressed with my cleaning skills! I won't let you down, boss!" Lucas threw out his hand and waited for his boss to shake it.

The man chuckled. "I'm sure you won't. You're doing a great job here, Luc. Always know that."

Feeling like he had just won the lottery, Lucas turned and darted from his boss's office.

Holy. Shit! He couldn't believe that that had just happened.

See what happens when you take a chance? that voice inside his head said.

Lucas couldn't stop smiling. He picked up a case of beer and carried it out to the front of the bar. Caden was busy unloading the bar's weekly beer delivery, so Lucas figured he would help the guy out by bringing a case or two out to the front bar.

He was in a fantastic mood, after all.

The front of the bar was empty. Alexis was probably off helping the guys with the delivery or something.

Smiling to himself, Lucas placed the case of beer on the bar, then spun around, doing a single ballerina pirouette turn.

A tiny voice giggled.

Eyes shooting open, Lucas stared down at a little girl with golden hair and two matching pigtails.

"Oh! Where did you come from?" Lucas asked, striking a pose against the bar and totally pretending that he wasn't just twirling around and shaking his ass like a professional dancer.

The little girl giggled again.

"You're funny!"

Lucas stared at the strange little person sitting alone in a booth... in a bar... playing with some little plastic toys on the table.

Cautiously, he approached her, taking extra care in case

the little one was a physical manifestation of some ghost child sent to haunt the bar and all those who worked in it.

Oh, great. He had just agreed to work overnight, alone, in a spooky, haunted bar.

Yup, his life sucked.

"Tell me, child, what is your favorite television show?" For some reason, he felt the need to speak to the potential demon child in an old-time British accent. He watched her suspiciously, which only made her laugh even more.

This was the most peculiar spawn of Satan he had ever encountered. Not that he had ever encountered ghost children before, but he assumed that television provided an accurate representation of how one would look and act if ever encountered.

"*Bluey*, of course," the little girl finally answered. She held up a tiny plastic figurine that kind of resembled an annoying blue dog.

"Hmm," Lucas said, rubbing his chin with his fingers as he pretended to analyze his mysterious visitor. "And what about *Paw Patrol*? Is that still a thing?"

"I'm too old for *Paw Patrol*, silly," the little girl answered, proving once again that Lucas knew nothing.

"Nonsense, you're never too old for laughter!" Lucas pretended to slip and fall to the ground, landing in the splits.

The child erupted into laughter. She stood up on the seat and began jumping up and down.

Probably not the safest thing for a child to be doing.

Neither was sitting alone... in a bar.

Climbing to his feet, Lucas pretended to rub his sore

back. "Wow, how clumsy of me. Someone must have spilled some water!"

The girl continued to giggle, clapping her hands and still jumping up and down.

Lucas reached out and took the young girl's little hand. "Tell me, sweet child, what is your name?" Still using a British accent.

He gently pulled the girl back down until her butt was once again safely planted in the comfy seat.

A seat, now covered in footprints.

It's good that the bar had just hired a specialized cleaner who could easily take care of cleaning up such messes.

"Elizabeth. But everyone calls me Lizzy."

"Well, sweet Lizzy. My name is Lucas, but everyone calls me Luc for short." He was back to his original voice as he slid onto the bench across from her. "So, tell me, Lizzy, does your mom or dad work here in the bar?"

The little girl nodded, her pigtails flopping around like they were doing an interpretive dance or something.

"Does your mom or dad have a name?"

"Yes. Dad."

Only a child could say that without a laugh. In all honesty, it wasn't until Luc was ten that he learned his parents were not named "Mom" and "Dad." Talk about earth-shattering news. He felt like his whole life had been a lie up until that point.

Sorry, little girl. You have a lifetime of disappointments and heartaches ahead of you.

"Is your daddy Nikolai?" He seemed like the type who would have a child in every state.

Although there was also Jake. No doubt there was probably a child or two floating around somewhere on the West Coast. No, wait. Jake liked to finish on a girl's tits. Ask him how he knew that one.

Lucas suddenly felt dirty. How long would it be before he could go home and wash the disgusting thoughts out of his brain?

The girl giggled.

Perhaps the little thing really was a demon. So far, he felt scared and a little grossed out.

"No. My daddy is Cade."

Lucas's breath caught in his chest as he stared across at eyes that matched the same shade of blue as his hero.

Caden has a daughter? He didn't realize that Cade was seeing anyone.

"Are you behaving, Lizzy?" Caden asked, carrying in two cases of beer at a time—like any self-respecting muscleman would.

"Of course I am, Daddy! I'm just talking to my new friend, Luc!"

Caden placed the cases down on the bar next to Lucas's measly one. "Are you now, pumpkin?" Caden gave Lucas a mischievous little smirk.

Yup! Definitely the daughter of a demon.

"Did you know that he can do the splits?" Lizzy cried out. "He can even do a funny dance."

This seemed to amuse Caden to no end.

"Oh really? And why have I never been subjected to your hilarious dancing?"

Lucas blushed.

"I only share those dances with my closest friends." Lucas gave a wink to Lizzy.

"Okay, now I feel jealous." He slid in next to his daughter and began tickling the side of her ribs.

The shriek that followed could raise the dead.

Lucas flinched, then started laughing at the pure joy and excitement emanating from Caden's daughter.

There was pure love there between father and daughter.

Seeing their connection made Lucas miss his own mom and dad, who were living and working down in Peru. He hadn't talked to them in ages and wondered how they were doing. He might even miss his sister—just a bit. She lived in the US, but they weren't very close either. Perhaps if he had been closer to his family, he wouldn't be in the predicament he currently found himself in.

Turning his gorgeous face toward Lucas, Caden gave him a heartfelt smile. "Luc, this here is the greatest love of my life: my daughter, Lizzy."

Lucas couldn't help but smile. "It's a pleasure to meet you, Lizzy. And thank you for keeping me company while your father was in the back!"

Elizabeth's smile nearly swallowed her face. "It was my pleasure, *funny dancing man!*"

Luc had a feeling that the name was going to stick. *Damn it.*

With that horrifying thought in mind, he got up from

the table, walked around to the other side of the bar, and began placing the beers into the fridge.

10

CADEN

O ver the next two weeks, Caden watched as Lucas came out of his shell. He seemed to be more comfortable and talkative, even laughing and joking with the guys at work. He still shied away from men who were big and bulky, but with people like Ace and Alexis, he really seemed to warm.

Caden, unfortunately, was still one of those people who Lucas got awkward around. He seemed to get tongue-tied and was never able to hold eye contact with Caden for very long. Seeing the boy blush and then quickly scurry away was both endearing and frustrating.

He wanted to get to know the boy better but found it difficult when he kept running away. Caden had half a mind to tie the guy down and force him to have a conversation... but with today's forceful confinement laws, holding someone against their will was kind of frowned upon.

All joking aside, Cade tried his best to make Lucas feel

more comfortable around him. He gave him head nods, tried to strike up conversations, and even went so far as to stay late after his shift to help the boy clean up the back storage room. All that managed to do was provide them both with thirty minutes of awkward conversation. No matter how hard he tried, each attempt seemed to end in failure.

He wasn't sure what the kid's issue was, but he hoped that with time, he might relax and let him in.

Monday nights were another slow time at the bar, so Caden and Nikolai rotated working the shift. Tonight was Caden's night off.

Bored, Caden decided to walk down to Betty's Diner and grab a burger for a late-night dinner. It was half past nine, and the place was mostly empty. Another slow night, it seemed.

Walking into the diner, Caden scanned the room, trying to decide where he wanted to sit. He pretty much had his pick of the place.

Just as he was about to sit down in an empty booth, he noticed a head of light-brown hair hunched over while reading a book.

Was that?

Smirking, Caden strutted on over to the table at the far end of the diner and stopped once he reached the table.

"Taking your book boyfriend out for dinner?" Caden asked, leaning against the side of the booth, arms crossed against his chest, biceps flexed.

He'd been adding a bicep flex to his stance since he was seventeen and realized that people were attracted to his muscles. He did it so often now that he didn't even take gender into account when posing.

A confused Lucas looked up, mouth slightly askew as his eyes focused on the person interrupting his dinner date.

"Cade? Wh-what are you doing here?"

Was it surprise or disappointment that he heard in Lucas's voice?

He hoped the first.

"Came in to do some laundry. How about you?"

He watched as the boy's face became even more confused. It was only after a few seconds that Lucas suddenly realized that Cade was joking.

"You might have to wait a while. It's pretty busy in here tonight," Lucas responded with his own attempt at humor.

Caden looked around. Even the waitress behind the counter looked bored.

"Mind if I sit?"

Lucas motioned to the seat in front of him.

At least it didn't appear that the kid was going to get up and run this time.

"So what'cha reading?" Cade asked, sliding his butt into the seat across from him.

Lucas flipped over the cover, revealing some tattooed muscle biker dude giving the reader a look that said he was about to bend them over and fuck them hard against his bike.

Cade gave an approving nod.

"Well, if you're gonna fantasize about getting railed by a guy, best to make it a ripped biker dude. We got the moves and the stamina to make you see stars before you pass out from exhaustion when shooting your load." Cade watched as Lucas's eyes dilated. Clearly, the kid had a thing for built bikers.

"Umm." Blushing, Lucas put his bookmark back in his book and set it face down on the table next to him. "I-I like the story," he stuttered, looking like someone who'd just been caught watching porn instead of studying or doing their afternoon chores. "It's got a really good... plot."

"I'm sure it does. Any story involving an eight-inch cock and an eager young twink is bound to have a great... *plot*." Cade winked, loving the way that Lucas's cheeks flushed even more than they had just moments ago.

There was something sweet and endearing about watching the boy blush and squirm.

"It does. This series has a great storyline... as well as some really hot... steamy scenes." Lucas let out a chuckle. "Shut up. It's not like you don't read *girlie* magazines for their riveting... *plots*."

Another smile.

Caden shrugged his shoulders. "I can't help it. The suspense of turning that page and wondering just how big the woman's knockers are going to be has me just..."

"Can I get you gentlemen anything?" the bored waitress from behind the counter asked, completely ruining the back-and-forth banter they had finally established.

The bitch was getting no tip.

"Just a burger and fries for me. How about you, *Mr. Romance*?"

Lucas's cheeks flushed once again.

Why was all this teasing so much fun?

"I'll just have a minestrone soup, please."

Caden frowned at the boy.

"Where's the meat? Where's the carbs?"

"There are carbs in the pasta shells," Lucas noted.

Caden shook his head.

Perhaps the kid was on a tight budget. He should lay off the teasing.

"Oh, and two beers. No, wait, one beer and..." Caden's voice trailed off as he gestured toward Lucas, waiting for his response.

"Oh, nothing for me."

"Come on, Mr. Romance. I'm payin' for dinner. So let's get shit-faced, and you can tell me all the different ways Mr. Big Dick fucks his little twink in your book." Caden gave him a teasing smirk.

Lucas looked mortified. He almost felt guilty but actually didn't.

The boy finally turned toward the waitress, most likely realizing that the faster he ordered a drink, the faster she would leave, and his humiliation would end.

"I'll have a beer as well. Thanks."

The waitress gave a nod, then disappeared into the back of the diner.

"Okay, so tell me about your book," Caden asked, interlocking his fingers and leaning forward on the table. He felt like an eager young schoolboy about to learn all the cheat codes in his favorite video game.

Lucas raised an eyebrow as he stared at Caden awkwardly.

"Why would a straight man want to hear all about how some twink gets his hole stretched out by some bouncer at a biker bar?"

Now it was Cade's turn to blush.

"Really? It's about a bouncer?" What were the chances? And did this mean that Lucas wanted his— Then he noticed the evil smirk on Lucas's face. "You're pulling my leg."

Chuckling, Lucas leaned back in his seat and folded his arms across his chest.

"Smooth. So, fine. If you won't tell me about your hot and steamy sex book, then tell me a bit about yourself. Where are you from originally?"

Lucas's breath caught in his chest. He had a feeling that the boy was going to try and change the subject.

Cheesy diner music played quietly over the speakers as they sat in silence, staring at each other. Was Lucas ever going to trust him enough to open up and let him peek behind the curtain?

Appearing to come to terms with a difficult decision, Lucas leaned forward, interlocking his fingers on the table and lowering his gaze.

"Well, I'm from LA." His voice was low and sullen as if he feared being overheard.

Even if their waitress had overheard their conversation, Caden doubted that she had the interest or the technological savvy to repost their conversation online. Something told Caden that if the woman had a cell phone, it was likely one of those ancient flip phones that one could purchase at a gas station or corner store.

"Nice. I've been there a few times. Love the beaches and hot weather. So what made you decide to move?"

Lucas glanced up at Cade before lowering his gaze once again.

"A bad relationship." There was a momentary pause before he looked up and added, "A very bad relationship."

Caden studied Lucas's face for a moment, trying to decipher the pained expression he had on his face.

"I'm sorry to hear that. Can I ask who ended it?"

Caden wanted to be sympathetic, but he also wanted to understand more about Lucas. Was he running from trouble? Or trying to heal a broken heart? If it was just a broken heart, why all the secrecy and no background checks and stuff?

No. There had to be more to the story.

"I did," Lucas finally answered after the longest silence in conversation history. "I think he got the message that it was over when he woke up, and I had run off."

"Run off?" Caden was even more confused.

"My ex was not a nice man. He was possessive, physically and verbally abusive, and had it in his mind that I was his to be controlled. It got so bad that I knew there were only two ways for me to escape, either by ending my life or by running off in the night."

"Jesus," Caden gasped. He reached across the table and took Lucas's hand in his. He gave it a firm squeeze, hoping that Lucas could pull some of his strength and courage.

"I chose the latter. I spiked his whiskey one night with a crazy amount of sleeping pills, and when he finally passed out, I hopped on the first bus out of LA."

Squeezing Lucas's hand, Caden could feel his blood begin to boil. He hated bullies and people who took advantage of and hurt the little guys. That was something that he never put up with.

"Give me this asshole's name and address, and I'm going to go bash his fuckin' face in," Cade snarled.

He couldn't imagine anyone ever trying to hurt the sweet young man sitting across from him. This fucker deserved to get his face smashed in and his teeth knocked out. Perhaps, even have his nuts cut off. Clearly, he didn't know what being a man was all about.

Lucas shook his head. His hands began fidgeting with the corners of his steamy biker sex book.

"No. Please don't. Darryl is a dangerous man and has resources at his disposal."

"Is that why you've been working cash jobs and don't have a credit card?" Cade asked, realizing his mistake when it was too late. He felt his cheeks burn.

"What? How do you know that I don't have a credit card?"

Cade released Lucas's hand and leaned back in his seat. The music playing over the crackling speakers had changed to some sort of eighties cover band.

What was with the music in this place?

"When you first started working at Ride 'em Hard, I thought you were a criminal or on the run, so I shared my concerns with the big guy. He happened to mention that there might be other reasons why someone wouldn't want a background check done on them. I'm guessing that's also why you ditched your cell phone?"

Lucas nodded. His hair fell slightly over his eyes.

Caden couldn't believe how much Lucas was opening up to him. All awkwardness and nervousness had seemed to disappear from the boy. Perhaps all Lucas needed was a chance to get to know Caden outside of the bar setting.

"That would have been the easiest way for Darryl to find me. That, and through my credit card usage. So I took out a few grand from my account when I left and haven't touched a penny since."

"But how can this asshole get access to all that info without being your husband or joint on your accounts? Or was he?" Cade suddenly realized that he never asked whether Lucas and his ex were married.

"He's a cop. And a crooked one at that."

Now it was all beginning to make sense. Lucas's ex would have had all his buddies hunting down his ex in a matter of days if he'd tried to use any of his accounts or cell phone.

Caden reached over the table and squeezed Lucas's hand once again.

"You're under our protection now. That asshole is never going to hurt you again. I promise you that."

Strangely, he felt this intense need to shield and protect the young man sitting across from him. Yes, they hadn't known each other for very long, and this was probably one of the longest conversations he'd ever had with the guy, but something inside him wanted to protect him.

No matter what, no harm would ever come to this man, ever again.

"Here are your drinks. Your food will be out in a sec," the waitress announced, materializing out of thin air.

Cade had totally forgotten about their order. He'd need more than a few beers to calm himself after hearing this crazy story.

"Thank you, Cade. You and the guys at the bar have been so great to me."

"Well, you're one of us now. We all stick together and watch out for one another."

"I'm starting to see that," Lucas said with a smile on his face.

A few minutes later, the waitress brought out their orders.

"So, where is Lizzy tonight?"

Freezing mid-chew, Caden put aside his tentative murder plot for Lucas's ex and rejoined the conversation at the table.

"Oh, she's with her mom tonight."

"Your wife didn't want to join you for dinner?"

"What?" Caden asked, confused and a tiny bit lost. Then his brain caught up with the conversation. "No. Lizzy's mom and I aren't together. She's just a chick I fucked one night after having too many drinks at the bar. Amber decided to keep the baby, and I usually get to see Lizzy on weekends during the day and on alternating holidays. Amber is decent about letting me see Lizzy whenever I want, so I have it pretty good compared to some other single dads. I had her the other day at the bar because Amber needed someone to babysit for her while she went to an appointment."

Caden couldn't believe he was sharing all of this personal info with someone he barely knew. Usually, he never discussed his personal life or Lizzy and her mom. It was one of those "men don't share feelings with others" kind of things.

"Well, Lizzy seems like a really sweet kid."

"That's all her mom. Thankfully, she doesn't take after me." Caden let out a chuckle as he finished off the last of his fries.

Caden was one of those weird people who liked to eat his fries first before diving into his burger. Why let your fries get cold? Then they taste like shit, and all you have is a juicy burger.

"We both know that isn't true."

Caden glanced up at the man sitting across from him. His stomach felt fluttery.

Why was getting a compliment from the boy making his stomach feel all funny?

11

CADEN

*B*y the time they finished their meal, it was just after eleven thirty at night. Leaving the diner, Caden distracted Lucas by asking him more about his love of theater and what made him want to perform live on stage.

"I swear, there is something magical about bringing a song to life and watching all those around you get transported by your voice. Seeing a young child's face light up at their favorite song or seeing an adult wipe away a tear as they are consumed with emotion is one of the greatest feelings in the world."

"Well, I don't really know much about musicals or Broadway shows, so I can't exactly say I understand what you are sayin', but I could see being lost in your voice."

Lucas's smile dropped from his face.

Why did he make that last comment? He had been thinking about how cute and sweet Lucas's voice was when he got all animated talking about something that he was so passionate about, and then he went and made it all weird.

It was at that moment that Lucas finally realized that Caden was walking him home.

"Oh, um, so I should probably let you get back to your place anyway. I don't live much further from here." His voice was high-pitched and riddled with nerves.

"It's alright, Mr. Romance. It's dark and late, and I'd feel more comfortable making sure that you get home safe."

"No, no. It's fine. You don't have to..." Lucas began but stopped when Caden shook his head.

"Trust me; I only want to make sure that you get home safe. I won't invite myself in or keep you from getting your beauty rest or anything."

He watched as Lucas fought back a smile and shook his head in disbelief.

"*Fine*, this way," he said reluctantly. It was about time that Lucas realized he could be a stubborn bull when he wanted to be.

They continued on for another ten minutes before they came to Old Man Benson's farm. It had been a while since Caden set foot on the crazy old man's property. Not since he was in his late teens and trying to find a secluded place to have a few drinks with his friends.

Caden, of course, was not including the night he followed Luc home. That night never existed.

"So, you're renting a room from Old Man Benson?" Caden asked, staring at the primary property, not wanting to let on that he knew the truth about Lucas's living situation.

"Not exactly," Lucas said, turning to his right and continuing to walk toward the large, brown-and-red barn nestled behind the property. "Mr. Benson had the barn converted into a loft a few years ago. I rent that space from him."

Lucas pulled open the big barn doors and took a step to the side. "After you." He motioned for Caden to enter.

A moment later, the barn came to life when Lucas flipped on the lights.

"It's not much, but it's home until I can save up and afford a better place."

Standing inside the barn, the place didn't look half as bad as it had when he had been peeking in through the window the previous night.

Lucas had set up some twinkle lights along the windows and ladder leading up to the loft. Their light brought a sort of comfy feeling to the space.

On the main level were all the usual tools and machinery one might expect to find in a barn: pitchforks, shovels, a muck tub, and even feed buckets and hay nets. All of these items were neatly stored off to one side of the barn to provide Lucas with as much living space as possible.

Thankfully, the place didn't smell like horses or farm animals. Caden guessed that it had been quite a while since Old Man Benson used the barn for such a purpose.

"Do you want to stay for a beer? I could throw on a movie or something?"

Caden was surprised to be invited in. Perhaps the boy was beginning to warm up to him after all.

He smiled.

"Sure. That would be great."

Lucas grabbed two beers from the fridge and then led them up the ladder to the loft above.

The loft was small and simple. There was a tiny table for sitting and eating breakfast, a dresser with a mirror mounted on the wall, and a mattress resting on a hand-made wooden frame, clearly crafted by the landlord himself.

Caden glanced around the room.

There was no television or a couch to sit on to watch the movie.

"Where are we...?" Caden began before noticing Lucas sitting on his bed, opening his laptop.

Taking a sip of his beer, he walked around to the other side of the bed, then paused as he tried to calculate the best way of positioning himself so that they could both fit on the tiny bed.

Tilting his head to the right and then the left, Cade tried to imagine the position of their legs and arms, possibly even their heads... *if he just?*

"You going to stand there all night admiring my bedspread? Or are you going to join me here on the bed?" Lucas asked, glancing up from his laptop. "If you're afraid of touching me, I can pull up one of the chairs from the table." Lucas nodded toward the small table to their right.

Why was he hesitating? What did he care if Lucas's arm brushed up against his?

"No. No. I was just trying to figure out how you do

doggy style in this miniaturized bed." He decided to go with humor to disguise his awkwardness.

"Easy. Me on the bed on all fours, with the guy standing right where you are."

Caden's cheeks flushed as Lucas gave him a wink. The boy had a funny sense of humor when he relaxed and let his guard down.

He could do this. Lie skin-to-skin next to the one guy who seemed to make his dick hard for no apparent reason.

He was a bull. A tough, thirty-two-year-old biker dude who fucked loads of hot chicks and was secure in his manhood.

He had this.

Flopping down onto the bed, Caden relaxed and decided to just go with it.

"You know, sometimes you act all shy and nervous, then smutty stuff like that falls from your mouth," Caden teased.

"Oh, sorry. I used to be fun and flirty in another life." Lucas's voice was back to being soft and timid. "Sometimes my personalities get crossed accidentally."

Caden hated hearing the way Lucas spoke about himself. Clearly, he was struggling with being true to who he was while coping with the person this trauma had made him into.

People say our personalities are shaped by our environments and circumstances. Cade could see how a traumatic experience might make Lucas more guarded and cautious. He hoped that, over time, Lucas would learn to trust again and allow his true self to shine through once more.

Without thinking, Caden swung his leg over Lucas's

body, then pulled the little shit up against himself. If he was going to do this, he was going to do it right.

Holding Lucas firmly against his chest, Caden nestled his chin between Lucas's neck and shoulder and breathed him in.

"Never apologize for being who you are. You are sweet and funny and smell like apricots and vanilla." Caden chuckled. "The only thing you need to apologize for is giving a straight man a boner when you flirt with him."

Lucas let out an unrestrained laugh. "Now who's being all smutty?"

Caden chuckled. He loved seeing this side of Lucas—all relaxed and cheery. Listening to him laugh warmed his heart. Holding him close to his chest... well, that didn't feel too bad either.

Originally, he wanted to cuddle Lucas to make him feel safe and special, but holding him close now... he was kind of enjoying it.

Nestling up against Caden's body, Lucas opened a file on his laptop containing movies and began scrolling through them.

"So, which one do you feel like watching?"

Honestly, he really didn't care. So long as he could continue to hold Lucas in his arms, they could watch paint dry for all he cared.

Once they finally decided on a movie, Lucas pressed play and linked his finger with Caden's across his stomach.

"Hey, Cade?"

"Hmm?"

"Thanks for being so cool and holding me like this tonight. I know that you're straight, and it must be awkward as hell sitting here like this for you. But I really miss being held by a man and feeling safe like this. Even if it doesn't mean anything to you, the gesture means a lot to me."

Feeling his heart swell, Caden tightened his arms around the body of his new buddy.

"Anytime, dude. Don't tell the other guys, but sometimes, I miss cuddling too." He leaned forward and gently kissed the top of Lucas's head.

He felt Lucas's body tense for a moment before it relaxed once again into his own.

He had no idea why he kissed the top of his head. It just felt like a natural response to what they were doing. He hoped that it didn't make things awkward between them.

Seriously. What was happening to him? He'd never had feelings like these toward another dude before. Why now? Why Lucas?

The movie began to play, and within minutes, they had both forgotten about the awkward kiss and became lost in the comedy of the movie they were watching.

Sometime after midnight, Caden felt his lids become heavy, and his body drift off to sleep.

12

LUCAS

What the fuck is that massive thing pressing up against his back?

He knew what it was. It was the same thing that had been digging into his back for the past forty-five minutes.

Every once in a while, he would feel more blood flow into Caden's python as the damn thing got harder and harder.

Like seriously? How big was the fucking thing?

He was both in heaven and hell.

The porn star in him wanted to turn on over and swallow the man's gigantic piece of meat until he passed out from not breathing or choked to death on all the man's cum. Either way, a glorious way to spend his morning.

The logical, non-pervy side knew that the man was straight and would not appreciate a homo like himself pulling down his jeans and waking him with a blow job—no matter how fantastically great it might be. Some might even dare to call it *award-winning* if they gave out awards for blow jobs. Oh, wait. They do. You just have to be in the adult film industry to get one.

See? Torture.

Lucas closed his eyes and tried not to moan out loud as Caden pushed his dick further into his body.

God, he wanted his cock. Judging by the thickness and hardness, Caden appeared to be having one hell of a sex dream.

Then, Caden's body froze.

Lucas felt Caden's body stiffen, a clear sign that he had just woken up and realized his predicament.

"Fuck," Caden whispered under his breath.

Should he let Caden know that he was awake? Or should he just continue to pretend that he was still sleeping and not make Caden feel any more uncomfortable than he probably already did?

"Classy, Cade. The guy finally lets his guard down and begins to trust you, and here you are, pressing your god-damn boner up against the poor guy's back."

Lucas couldn't hold in his giggle.

"And, of course, you're awake."

"Sorry, it's hard to sleep when you got the world's largest dick threatening to impale your spleen."

"It's not the world's largest," Caden said, stretching and digging his dick into Lucas's back even more unintentionally.

His body jerked back. "Fuck, sorry," Caden apologized when he realized what he was doing. He shifted in the bed, still cuddling Lucas but no longer jamming his dick into him.

"Sorry, I fell asleep. Didn't mean to sleep over."

Rubbing the hair on Cade's forearm, Lucas lay there, enjoying the feel of Caden's chest rising and falling against his body. He knew that nothing romantic could ever come of this, but still, he was enjoying the warmth of Caden's body pressed firmly against his own.

"It's cool. I fell asleep as well and didn't realize."

"What time is it?" Cade asked, his voice still heavy with sleep.

Lucas glanced at the clock that hung against the wall.

"It's six thirty in the morning."

A groan escaped Cade's throat. "Why are we up at *ass-crack* o'clock?" He rolled onto his back with his arm still trapped under Lucas's body.

Chuckling, Lucas rolled over, placing his hand on Cade's chest as he stared up into his sleepy blue eyes.

"Well, I was trying to sleep, but something kept poking me, asking if I wanted to play." He chuckled. He knew that he was being flirty, and it probably wasn't smart, considering the guy was six-two, straight, and could probably bench-press triple his body weight. He was just begging to get gay-bashed.

But he did fall asleep cuddling you, and he hasn't run off just yet, so what does that say?

It says that Lucas was horny as hell and would use any logic possible to get this man's dick into his mouth.

Caden lifted his head and gazed down at the bulge in his jeans.

"Yeah, I swear the fucker has a mind of its own. Always popping up at the most inappropriate times." He lowered his head back onto the one pillow they shared and stared up at the rafters. With his left hand, he began caressing Lucas's shoulder.

What the...? Why was he?

Was this really happening? What sort of straight dude would start rubbing a gay man's shoulder while sporting a massive boner in bed?

Lucas could feel his own cock begin to thicken. He'd never been so turned-on before in his life.

He took a chance and glanced down at Caden's package. His zipper was stretched to the max as it struggled to contain the beast lurking beneath.

Perhaps it was just his imagination or wishful thinking, but Lucas swore he saw the damn thing throb as if it were getting harder as they spoke.

Swallowing hard, Lucas decided to take a chance and see if the signals he thought he was picking up on were real.

Slowly, he began sliding his hand down Caden's chest, over his rock-hard abs, and then stopped just above Caden's belt buckle. He glanced up at Caden, who now had his eyes closed. His lips were slightly parted as he slowly breathed in and out.

He wasn't sure. So far, Cade hadn't stopped his hand from sliding down, but what if he had fallen back asleep or if he was too scared to tell him he had misread the situation?

Should he just ask to make sure?

As if sensing his trepidation, Caden grabbed his hand and guided it to his belt buckle.

Okay, that was clearly a sign that he was willing to proceed.

Licking his lips, Lucas lifted the leather of Caden's belt, loving the sound of the metal as it released the confines of Caden's massive meat.

Once the buckle was undone, he moved on to the button of Caden's jeans. He popped it open slowly, then reached for the zipper that was begging to be released.

Trying to control his breathing, Lucas slid down Caden's zipper, cherishing every metal tooth as it slowly separated. With every notch open, he got closer to that massive package.

If Lucas had been asked what his top five sexual experiences had been, this would definitely be in the top two.

Licking his lips, he gently pulled back the folds of Caden's jeans.

Jesus. The man bulge was everything it had promised to be. Thick. Solid. And begging to be released from its confines.

Wanting to enjoy every possible moment, Lucas slowly ran his fingers along the surface of Caden's dick.

The man let out a moan. It was subtle and deep. Exactly the way Lucas imagined a questioning, straight man might moan when they first have their cock played with by another man. It was pleasurable yet nerve-wracking. Exciting yet terrifying.

Lucas needed this dick.

In his mouth.

Cutting off all sources of oxygen.

Struggling against the tight folds of Caden's boxer briefs, Lucas finally managed to pull Caden's dick out of his underwear.

"Fuck," Lucas groaned as he caught sight of the man's raging hard cock.

It was long and thick and had the most glorious mushroom head Lucas had ever seen. The guy could make a fortune doing gay porn if he wanted.

Slowly, Lucas began jerking the man's cock, loving how it throbbed in his hand as he moved up and down.

"Lube. Do you got any lube?" Caden whispered through shallow gasps of air. His eyes were still shut tight while his tongue wet his lower lip.

"Umm, yeah." Lucas quickly released Caden's cock, loving the heavy thump his dick made as it flopped back down against his lower abdomen.

Lucas quickly grabbed the well-used bottle of lube out of his top drawer and drained half the thing on Caden's shaft without thinking. His brain was still attempting to comprehend what was happening, that he was able to play with Caden's cock at all.

Gripping his shaft, Lucas began jerking his cock in long, even strokes. Once he reached the tip of Caden's dick, he'd twist his hand over the top giving the man a bit of extra motion on the downstroke.

The man let out a groan.

Lucas dared a glance up at Caden. His eyes were heated, staring down at Lucas as he played with his cock. With every stroke, Caden let out a sinful moan. Slowly, his lips began to part as if begging for more.

He knew what Caden needed—his balls to be emptied, without having to say the words out loud.

"God, this is so damn hot," Lucas whispered, leaning his body closer to Caden's as he continued his assault on the biker dude's cock.

Another moan.

Caden's grip on Lucas's shoulder tightened as his breathing began to increase.

Letting out a growl, Caden began fucking his dick into Lucas's tight fist.

The move was hot—Caden taking control of his own pleasure, eyes closed once again as he fucked his way toward his orgasm.

"That's it. Fuck that tight hole," Lucas moaned.

"Fuck, yeah," Caden whispered, digging his nails into Lucas's shoulder. His pumping became erratic. Switching between short, quick pumps, then moving into long, deep thrusts.

Jesus, Lucas's mind was about to come undone. Watching Caden use his hand for his own enjoyment had his mind short-circuiting. It was the single hottest thing he had ever witnessed.

"I'm... almost..." Letting out a final growl, Caden's body went stiff as warm streams of cum came shooting out of his cock.

Every muscle in Caden's abs tightened and flexed as he rode out his orgasm to completion.

Lucas's own cock pressed firmly against his jeans as he continued to jerk Caden's cock until his body stopped jerking and his balls were completely empty.

"Wow. That was quite the load." Lucas chuckled, loving the feeling of being painted with Caden's cum.

Talk about taking a *cum bath*. The man's load was everywhere! On Caden's chest, Lucas's shoulder, and even the wall above Lucas's bed.

"Fuck, that was hot," Lucas huffed out, still trying to catch his own breath.

Jerking off a man's dick was a lot of work, and one wouldn't believe how sore an arm could get, especially if the surface he was jerking was big.

And Caden's was big!

Hopping off his bed, Lucas quickly darted across the room to retrieve a small hand towel for cum cleanup.

When he turned back around, Caden was already out of bed, tucking his cock back in his jeans and fumbling, trying to do up his belt.

"Umm, don't you want to wipe off?" Lucas asked, holding up the hand towel.

"Umm. No, that's okay. I really need to get going. It's late, and I've got some things that I need to get done."

The man could not even make eye contact.

Fuck. He'd screwed up.

This was why he didn't fool around with straight guys. They never know what they want, and then they feel all guilty and weird and can't get the fuck out of your place fast enough.

"Cade, are you—" Lucas began before being cut off.

"Yeah, man. I just gotta run before I'm late." He pulled

down the back of his shirt and descended the ladder two steps at a time.

Lucas watched from the top of the loft as the hottest straight guy he had ever fooled around with rushed out of his place like he had the plague or something.

So much for a magical morning.

Fuck, why did he give in when he knew better?

Because you were lonely and horny, and for the first time in ages, you didn't feel ugly.

Argh!

13

CADEN

*C*aden ground his teeth for the fiftieth time that evening. At this rate, he wasn't going to have any teeth left by the end of his shift.

The sound of their laughter.

Watching the way he leaned in close and whispered God knows what into Lucas's ear.

Even watching the way he casually rubbed his hand along Lucas's inner thigh made Caden want to rip the little prick's throat out with his bare hands.

He wondered how long it would take for the little fucker to bleed out. Grasping at the gaping hole that once was his throat while Caden stood above him, happily enjoying the show.

No, he was not being overly dramatic, and no, he did not think he was being unreasonable. The guy was a douche and clearly only after one thing.

And what do you care if Mr. Douche sticks his prick into

that yummy piece of delicious pie? It's none of your business, is it? You're straight. He's gay. Gay men sleep with other gay men, and the last time I checked? Mr. Douche was gay. Very gay.

That annoying voice inside his head was right. Cade had no reason to care who Lucas decided to hang out with or who he let stick their dick into his body.

Caden was straight, and Lucas was gay.

It had been two weeks since Caden had freaked out and ran from Lucas's loft after receiving the best fucking hand job of his life. Seriously, his soul left his body as he was coming and only returned once Lucas released his grip.

It had also been two weeks since Caden began avoiding Lucas like the plague.

And people were starting to notice.

Caden hated the way he reacted. Once he came and his brain brought itself back online, he panicked.

He had no idea what to do or say or how he should be feeling.

Was he gay? Bi? Was he suddenly into dudes? All he knew was, at that moment, he wanted to be as close to Lucas as possible.

Listening to his breathing and feeling Lucas's warm skin pressed against his as he enjoyed every minute of playing with Caden's dick—it had all been so... intoxicating.

That was the best way to describe it. His senses were heightened, his skin felt electric, and his dick... well, it had never been so hard in his entire life.

It's true what they say about having cum fog on the brain. When you are horny and in the throes of passion, everything is fair game. But the second you shoot that load and the fog clears, you're suddenly bombarded with all the questions... all the emotions... that you should have considered before going and fucking everything up, chasing after a goddamn orgasm.

Caden could still see that horrified look on Lucas's face the moment he realized that Caden was leaving.

Charging out the door was more like it.

But what was he supposed to do? Lie there and cuddle? Talk about their feelings and braid each other's hair?

The truth was that he didn't know how he felt.

He had never had a desire to be with another man.

Now there he was, cuddling and kissing and even getting a hand job from another dude.

God, he was so confused.

Another burst of laughter came from the booth that Lucas shared with Ace and his friends, *dufus* and *douchebag*.

Caden had overheard Ace telling Lucas that he had a friend who was interested in Lucas and thought they could all hang out and have some drinks one night this week.

One night this week turned into two.

Was there going to be a third?

None of your damn business. You just spent the last two weeks ignoring the man you hooked up with and then ran away the second you busted your nut.

Classy, dude. Real classy.

"What's up with the dagger eyes?" Marcus asked, sliding in next to Caden at the bar. He followed his line of sight and gave a groan.

"What?" Caden asked, ignoring the annoying sound that happened to leave his boss's throat.

"What's up with you two? You guys have been acting weird these past two weeks. I thought you two were becoming friends?"

"We were—are. Nothing." Caden huffed. "I just don't like the way that punk is fondling Lucas under the table."

"Fondling? The guy's twenty-four. And judging by the smile on Lucas's face, I get the feeling he's enjoying the handy going on under the table."

Caden glared at his boss.

"Whatever. They should have a bit of respect for this place and at least take it to the restroom or back alley like everyone else."

Marcus let out a chuckle. "Weren't you the one fingering that redhead on the pool table last Fourth of July?"

He had no idea what the chick's name was. She had been traveling through town with her girlfriends when they decided to stop in for a drink. If he remembered correctly, Nikolai showed her friend where the ladies' bathroom was while Caden kept her company in the bar.

"That was different. I was helping her out with an itch that she couldn't reach. You know. Good customer service and all."

Another snort from his boss. "Always the model employee."

Across the bar, Lucas's date slid out of the booth and headed toward the bathroom.

"I need to take a piss," Caden grumbled, standing from

his seat and stomping off toward the restroom. He ignored Marcus's warnings not to kill any of his customers.

He wasn't concerned. There would always be bodies to fill empty seats in a bar. People were turning twenty-one every day.

Once Caden entered the restroom, he spotted Lucas's date taking a piss at the urinals. Of course the jackass was ignoring men's room etiquette and was pissing in the center urinal. *Fuck that bastard.*

Caden stepped up to the urinal right next to the douchebag and unzipped his jeans. He fished out his cock, giving it a quick tug to stretch the guy out to its full hanging potential.

No matter what guys say, they are always competing to have the biggest dick at any urinal. It's in their DNA.

Letting out a slow breath, Caden relaxed his body and let the river begin to flow.

"So, you must be the new boyfriend," Caden growled, staring ahead at the tile on the wall. He didn't have to scope out the competition. He knew that his dick was already way bigger than *Little Miss Douchebag's.*

"Excuse me?" the boy asked, confused and turning his head slightly.

Caden caught him glancing down before snapping his head back toward the wall in front of him.

Caden smirked. *Guess there's no doubt about who the true alpha is in this scenario.*

"Lucas. I assume that you two are dating. This is the second time you guys have been out on a date this week."

The boy smiled. "Ya, he's smoking hot, and I would love to get him down on his knees, but no, we are not dating. *Yet.*"

There was something predatorial about the way the *douchebag* spoke. Perhaps it was all in Caden's head, but either way, he didn't like the thought of Lucas getting down on his knees for this beta. Lucas deserved an alpha. A man who could protect him and give him exactly what he needed inside and outside of the bedroom.

Too bad you're straight, that voice inside his head said, taunting him and reminding him that he had no place in Lucas's life.

Caden shook his cock before turning to face his new nemesis. He tucked his dick back into his jeans, reminding the punk who the true alpha was in this scenario.

"Yes, Lucas is a great guy and sexy as hell. Which is why I thought it was important for me to introduce myself. I'm Caden, Lucas's... friend. I'm also very protective of my friends. So if I catch you doing anything... *inappropriate* or mistreating the guy in any way..." Caden did up his fly and fastened his belt buckle. "Me and my brothers will take you out back and break every bone in your body."

The pipsqueak swallowed hard as he listened intently.

"Do we have an understanding?" Caden asked, flexing his muscles as he glared at the boy metaphorically pissing his pants.

The boy nodded.

"Good. You should also probably say your goodbyes and

call it a night. Lucas has a lot to do tomorrow, so he needs his rest."

The man nodded, still standing at the urinal holding his dick. He'd stopped pissing a few minutes ago but seemed to be in some sort of frozen state.

"Oh. And I don't need to tell you to keep this little conversation between us. My brothers and I hate it when our private conversations are shared with others. And how much more private can a conversation be than one standing at the urinals while holding our dicks in our hands."

"Got it. Between us."

"Good boy," Cade said before moving to wash his hands. "Nice chatting with you, *little dude*," he said while pushing open the bathroom door and leaving.

Across the bar, Caden watched as *Mr. Douchebag* slinked back to his table. He whispered something into Lucas's ear before waving to the others and then making his way to the door.

Lucas shook his head as if confused by the man's sudden departure. Ace reached across the table and squeezed his hand.

Caden hated to see such disappointment on the boy's face, but that loser wasn't good enough for him. Lucas needed someone confident and strong, someone who wasn't afraid to walk up to a person taking a leak and threaten their life. Someone who would do whatever it took to protect him and always keep him safe.

What about love and care for him? that pesky voice inside his head asked.

Yeah, that too. That was sort of a given.

Or was it because it's only strength and protection that you can offer the guy? That's why you only mentioned those two attributes.

I care for the guy. I bought him a friggin cell phone and walked him home late at night. Even now, I'm making sure that he doesn't get hurt by losers like Mr. Crooked Dick Man.

And yet you're willing to let Lucas believe that the guy left because of something that he did.

That wasn't my intention.

No. It wasn't, was it?

Caden let out a growl before deciding it was time to resume his duties and guard the front door. He was the protector of this bar, not only the people he cared about inside it.

14

CADEN

The next day, Marcus asked Caden and Blade to drive down to Houston and pick up an order of guns that had finally arrived.

In addition to working at the bar, the crew also worked side jobs as part of the Shadow Vipers. The biker gang participated in the usual transport of guns or drugs for local criminal organizations. They also offered additional muscle or protection when jobs became heated or gangs were hesitant to trust one another. Basically, they went where the money was.

If Caden had to guess, he assumed that sixty percent of Marcus's cash came from Vipers business while the remaining forty came from the bar. Of course, he had no real idea. All financials were taken care of by Marcus and his brother, Ace, but judging by some of the merchandise and services the Vipers provided, Caden was pretty sure that his estimates were not very far off.

Ride 'em Hard was the perfect cover for Marcus's illegal activities. The bar provided a way for him to launder his money while making it appear that his cash was from legitimate sources.

Bars were a cash-intensive business, so it was hard for the IRS to distinguish which deposits were related to the sale of alcohol and which were from the sale of trafficked guns.

Today, they were picking up a couple of cases of 9mm semiautomatic handguns for a street gang known as *The Scorpion's Kiss*. They were a newer gang that was starting to gain power and street credibility in Phoenix, Arizona.

The guns had their serial numbers filed off and were untraceable if ever used in a crime. The guns had been fitted with minor alterations the gang had specifically asked for.

Who knew that even gang leaders were picky about their hardware?

Marcus had met the leader of the gang a year ago while visiting some friends in Phoenix. His crew was then contracted to help with supplying weapons and security transports for a few of the higher-end drug runs the gang completed from time to time. State troopers weren't as confident pulling over a pack of bikers cruising along the interstate.

These gigs were becoming bigger and more high-risk as the years progressed. It was clear that Marcus was working on building a name for the crew, and judging by their clientele, Marcus's crew was really starting to make a name for themselves.

They were a crew that could be relied upon and trusted

to deliver. Discretion was always assured. And, of course, if you tried to betray the Shadow Vipers... let's just say, people would be finding your body parts all across the desert.

No, Marcus's crew was not to be messed with.

It was just after three a.m. when Caden pulled the minivan into the parking lot at the back of the bar and began carrying crates of merchandise down into the basement.

Marcus had installed a fake wall with a hidden room to store their less-than-legal merchandise. Only select members of the crew knew about this storage room. Marcus believed that the fewer people who knew where the merchandise was stored, the less risk there was of the authorities finding out or the items being stolen. Not that people were dumb enough to steal from Marcus. That was just absurd.

Caden and Blade were among those who knew about the storage room. Both had been working with Marcus since they were nineteen.

Since the room was hidden, a security lock or access code was not needed to gain entry. One just had to know how to access the unlocking mechanism that allowed the wall to be opened.

Reaching for the broken lamp attached to the wall, Caden turned the fixture left and pulled the wall forward once he heard the lock disengage.

Caden and Blade spent the next twenty minutes unloading the merchandise. It was tiring, but the fewer people who knew about this room, the more secure their business would be.

"There. I think that's it." Caden huffed, placing the last

case neatly against the wall and filling out the inventory log that Ace insisted they keep.

"We need to know what orders have been placed and picked up and what is still outstanding. Personally, I don't want to get a bullet in my ass because I forgot to deliver someone's order," Ace once scolded when Caden had forgotten to update the inventory log.

Cade returned the log to its spot on the cabinet and glanced around at all the items "pending delivery."

There were guns and ammo, and knives that were illegal in the States, but collectors craved to have them as part of their collection. There were even exotic animals, such as rare lizards and spiders—thank god Marcus tended to those items himself. There were even a few snakes that a mad scientist had asked them to procure for him. He claimed that he was conducting experiments using their venom, but people were weird, so who knew why the man was really asking for the creatures?

Frankly, Caden wasn't sure why the man couldn't go out and capture his own snakes. It's not like these ones were illegal, but perhaps the man had a fear of handling snakes. Either way, that was what kept the money rolling in. Getting things for people that they normally couldn't get on their own.

"Sounds good, boss," Blade responded, heading back up the stairs with Caden in tow.

When they reached the top of the stairs, Caden closed the door and then froze in his tracks.

Music was playing at the front of the bar.

"What's that?" Blade asked, pulling a gun from the inside of his jacket and tiptoeing toward the unknown source.

"Wait. Let me check it out first. You're liable to shoot someone's head off accidentally," Caden ordered. He found it unlikely that a robber would break into the bar and then blast music for everyone to hear.

Caden slowly pushed open the back room door and peeked into the main area of the bar. All the bar lights were on, and a tiny, brown-haired twink was dancing in the middle of the room, holding a mop and belting out the lines to a show tune that sounded vaguely familiar.

"What the fuck?" Blade whispered, peering over Caden's shoulder with a shit-eating grin that practically swallowed his head.

Grinning, Caden watched as Lucas twirled around the room, belting out lyrics about seasons of love.

The boy was magical. Listening to the depth of emotion and pain in his voice as he sang formed a lump in Caden's throat that he struggled to swallow.

The song was about love and loss and measuring one's worth over a lifetime. Was it measured in truths learned or times that were cried? The song seemed to describe the various seasons of love. Hearing it sung in Lucas's voice gave Caden goose bumps.

Was this what Lucas was talking about when he mentioned transporting people to another world and causing them to feel such emotions? The boy was right. Seeing Lucas perform was like watching a butterfly emerge from its cocoon.

It was both magical and life-altering.

Beside him, Blade was recording the performance on his cell phone, no doubt to benefit him at a later date.

"Who knew that the boy could sing?" Blade whispered over Caden's shoulder.

He didn't want to disturb the boy. Watching Lucas perform was like nothing he had ever witnessed before.

"He went to school for musical theater," Caden heard himself say.

"And now he's working at a dump like this?"

Caden jabbed Blade in the ribs with his elbow. "How about you head home and keep this little performance to yourself?" Caden suggested, giving his buddy a "this is not up for negotiations" glare.

"Sure thing, boss," the young man answered, locking his cell phone and shoving it back into his jeans.

Over his shoulder, he listened as Blade slipped out the back door and drove away.

He wanted to keep watching but knew that he was now standing in creepy stalker territory once again.

The song finally ended with Lucas striking a pose.

Caden took this as his opportunity to announce his presence. He began clapping as he walked into the main room.

Startled, Lucas let out a yelp and spun around quickly, eyes wide with terror.

"Damn, who knew you had a voice like that?" Caden cheered, making his way over to where Lucas was standing.

The look of shock and surprise quickly faded, only to be replaced with something much more... *unfriendly*.

Dipping his mop back in the water bucket, Lucas turned his back on Caden and resumed mopping the floors.

"What the hell are you doing here, *creeper*?" Lucas huffed under his breath.

Well, that was a little more hostile than he was expecting.

Smirking, Caden stepped over the wet spot on the floor and leaned against the bar.

"Had to drop something off for the big man. What are *you* doing here?" He hoped that perhaps some witty banter might lighten the mood.

"What does it look like, Sherlock?"

Ouch, someone had their panties all up in a bunch.

"Well, it looked like you were performing on Broadway."

Lucas's head snapped up, clearly not happy to see Cade in his space. He didn't blame him. After running off and then ignoring him for two weeks, was he really expecting a warm welcome?

"Sorry," Caden apologized. "You sounded really good singing, by the way."

The mop stopped moving. Lucas straightened up before turning to glare at Caden.

"I don't get it. You spent the last two weeks ignoring me; now you pretend like we are besties chilling in a bar?"

Caden felt like shit. Everything Lucas was saying was true. He had acted like an immature coward and tried to play it off as no big deal.

"Sorry. You're right."

"About which part?" Lucas asked, placing his hand on his hip like a parent scolding their child.

"All of it." Caden lowered his head, ashamed of how he had reacted.

"You just ran off!"

Caden lifted his head. "What?"

"That night, after I gave you that hand job, you just ran off. Which, by the way, made me feel real fucking good about myself. Then you proceeded to ignore me for the next two weeks! Jesus, Cade. I get that you're straight and that it freaked you out being with a dude, but I figured I at least deserved an explanation. A quick, 'Sorry, Luc, but fooling around with dudes is not my thing.' That was all you needed to do. At least that way, I wouldn't have spent the last two weeks feeling like the biggest asshole in the world hitting on a straight dude."

Hearing the pain in Lucas's voice cut deep. He hadn't realized just how vulnerable Lucas had been and how much his actions had hurt him.

"You're right, and I'm sorry. I did freak out. When I came, I wasn't sure how I felt. Part of me really enjoyed what we had just done, and another part of me wondered what it all meant. I wasn't ready to have those conversations with you, so I panicked. The only thing I could think of was to run. Get out of there as fast as I could until I could figure out what it all meant. So, you're right. I handled that poorly, and for that, I'm truly sorry."

Warm, sympathetic eyes stared back at Caden. He didn't seem like he wanted to kill Caden anymore, so that had to be a good thing.

Lucas stepped forward, still holding the mop in his hand.

"Look, I get that what we did was confusing, but you also have to realize that that was the first time I had been with a man... since my ex."

Understanding washed over Caden. That night had also been confusing as hell for Lucas. He had also been battling with his own emotions and demons, struggling to make sense of it all. Lucas simply managed to handle it all a lot better than Caden did.

"Next time, just talk to me like an adult." Lucas's voice was both tired and frustrated.

"Fair enough." He wondered if there would ever be a next time.

He still hadn't processed what all of these new feelings actually meant. He wished that he were able to talk to someone, but he really couldn't. Not unless he wanted to risk outing himself to the entire crew. That was if he ended up being bi or one of the other letters in that queer rainbow.

Caden looked around the room. There were cleaning products and garbage bags everywhere. "So, do you want to tell me what it is that you are doing here?"

Lucas looked around the room as well. "Marcus agreed to give me a few extra shifts a week to do a deep clean of this place. It gives me a few extra bucks in pay and makes this place look less... *depressing biker bar* in the end."

Caden hopped to his feet and rolled up his sleeves. "Okay, put me to work."

"Sorry, can't do. I need to do this work on my own. If Marcus suspects that I am getting someone to help me, I won't get paid the same, or he'll cancel my extra shifts. Thanks for the offer though."

"In that case." Caden looped around the bar and pulled a bottle of vodka and a few mixers off the shelves, grinning. "I'm going to make myself a drink. Want one?"

Lucas looked over at where Cade was busy pouring liquids into a shaker.

"I don't think the boss will be happy with you drinking all his booze."

"I'm not," Caden said, dropping a twenty into the register before finishing mixing his drink. "Did I ever tell you that I've always wanted to be a bartender? I've always loved mixing drinks."

He set out two glasses and then proceeded to pour the liquid from the shaker into them.

"Normally, I'd add a few garnishes to make the glass look all pretty and shit, but everything is all cleaned and locked up for the night. Here, try this."

Caden passed Lucas his red concoction and watched as Lucas cautiously brought the glass to his lips and took a sip.

"Mmm! That's really good!" Lucas praised, lifting his glass and staring at the liquid. "It almost tastes watermelon-y."

"Good guess. I'm still working on perfecting the drink, but when it's all done, you can help me name it."

Lucas smiled.

"Have you ever thought about asking Marcus if you can bartend for him? Even if it's just for a few nights of the week," Lucas asked, taking another sip from his drink.

Caden blushed. That was the big question he had always been too afraid to ask.

What if the man said no? Was he even good enough to bartend?

"Nah. I'm not good enough to do this for a living. Plus, with arms like these," Caden flexed his biceps, "I make the perfect bouncer."

Always just a piece of meat and nothing more than hired muscle.

While it may have come across as a joke, secretly, Caden hated himself. If he didn't feel that he was worthy enough to be more than Marcus's hired muscle, why would he expect others to think differently?

Pushing that thought from his mind, he glanced back up at Lucas.

"Okay, you get back to cleaning, and I'll just sit here enjoying my drink." Caden gave him a wink as he plopped his meaty ass down on a barstool.

He would hang out and keep the boy company for the night, hoping to get back into his good graces. He really enjoyed hanging out with Lucas at the diner and then again after for their little movie night. He felt horrible about the way he had reacted and hoped to somehow find his way back into Lucas's trusted circle.

Slowly, over time, he would eventually earn his way back.

For now, he would sip his drink and watch a cheerful Lucas as he wiped down furniture and mopped up the floor.

It wasn't long before Lucas returned to his one-man

Broadway performance, belting out another Broadway tune he had never heard of. It sounded nice and cheery.

There was so much life in the boy once he let himself relax and lower his walls. His true self was starting to show.

If this was what Lucas looked like, always smiling, always singing, Caden never wanted to see another frown on the boy's face again.

15

CADEN

*T*wo nights later, Caden found himself walking by Ride 'em Hard once again. It was just after two thirty in the morning, and the bar was closed up for the night.

Closed but not empty.

Standing by the front window, he grinned as he watched Lucas throw his arms up into the air before crouching down into some kind of shimmy. It must have been some sort of dance move from some musical he had never heard of.

Whatever it was, it was fun, upbeat, and full of life.

Just like Lucas.

More and more, he found Lucas invading his thoughts. He had never met anyone quite like him. His spirit, his cheerful demeanor. He had come a long way from that timid, shy young man who bumped into him while exiting the bathroom.

It still took a bit of time for Lucas to warm up to large,

rough-looking men, but you could see him struggling to try. Whatever his ex had done to him had really fucked him up mentally and emotionally. But Lucas would get there in time.

Rapping on the window, he waved when Lucas spun around, startled. His face lit up when he caught sight of Cade.

"Don't you ever sleep?" Lucas asked as he pushed open the front door.

Caden shrugged. "I was busy cleaning and changing the sheets on Lizzy's bed. She's coming to stay with me for the next three days."

"Oh, that's exciting!" Lucas cheered, stepping back and letting Caden through the door. "So what do you have planned?"

Caden shrugged. "Probably order a pizza, then play some video games. The girl's obsessed with *Mortal Kombat*. She can kick my ass any day."

The bar smelled like pine-scented cleaner. It wasn't a bad smell, but it was definitely a smell that customers and the guys at the bar would not be used to. Normally the bar smelled of liquor, sweat, and horny desperation.

"How often do you play?" Lucas asked as he reached over a booth and began running down the wood with a rag that was no longer white.

Jesus, how dirty was this fuckin' place?

"Usually once or twice a week, depending on how often I get her."

Lucas paused as if trying to comprehend what Caden had just said.

Lucas straightened up.

"Here's a thought. The day after tomorrow, the library is hosting a *Hairspray* movie sing-along night in the park behind the library. Why don't you bring Lizzy? I'm sure she would love it."

"*Hairspray*? What's that?"

Lucas's mouth dropped open before closing suddenly as if he had answered his own question.

"Sorry, for a second there, I forgot that you were straight and not one of my theater friends." Lucas chuckled. "Trust me. Your daughter will love it! There is big hair, lots of color, and John Travolta in a dress!" Lucas exclaimed, using his hands to indicate "big hair" above his head.

Now it was Caden's turn to chuckle.

"Basically, the kids can dress up if they want, they watch the movie and sing and dance and get to eat popcorn and candy, and basically expel a shit ton of energy before they have to go to bed."

Cade smirked. "Hmm, I like the tiring my kid out part of it." Plus, it would be fun watching his little munchkin running around singing her little heart out.

"Okay, we'll do it. But on one condition."

"What's that?" Lucas asked, applying more cleaning solution to the disgusting brown-and-black rag that he was using to clean the backside of the furniture.

Who knew you had to clean all sides of chairs?

"You have to come with Lizzy and me to the sing-along."

Lucas's head snapped toward Cade.

"Me? No. No. This is daddy and daughter time."

"But I thought you would love it?" Caden asked, confused and feeling a bit rejected. Normally, girls jumped at the opportunity to join him for a night out.

But usually, those were dates, his inner voice explained.

Yeah, but... still.

He liked Lucas and wanted to spend more time with him, and he knew that this was something that Lucas would love to do.

"Oh, don't worry. I plan on being there. Front row and center. Dancing and singing and wearing my big blue wig."

Lucas was beaming with excitement.

"See? You will already be going. So why not join Lizzy and me and show us how a real professional does it?"

Eyes locked on his, Lucas appeared to be assessing the situation.

Was Lucas worried that he would freak out again and run off? Was he worried that people might find it strange that the two of them—two dudes, one gay, one straight—were hanging out together at a... *musical*?

"You really sure you want me intruding on your time with your daughter?" Lucas asked, appearing unsure.

"Of course. She loves you."

Walking around the bar, Caden began pulling bottles down from the shelf before grabbing a shaker and two glasses.

"Come on. I won't take no for an answer. I'll even butter you up with one of my special blue lemon drop martinis. You'll love it."

Without waiting for an answer, Caden began mixing

liquids into the aluminum shaker before popping on the lid and shaking it vigorously.

Caden pretended not to notice the way Lucas's pupils dilated as they locked onto Caden's biceps while he shook.

Okay. He knew that he was being a cocktease, but who was he to deny the man a good look at a sex god in action? He spent hours at the gym each week, trying to sculpt that perfect body. A body that people could enjoy and salivate over.

Lucas licked his bottom lip without realizing it.

Yeah, the boy was hooked.

"Well, okay. On one condition. You ask Lizzy's mom if she is comfortable with one of your friends joining her daughter at one of these events. It's always important that both parents are consulted before any strangers are allowed to interact with their kids."

"But Lizzy already met you in this bar?" Caden protested, not really sure what the big deal was anyway.

"Yeah, and that was Daddy mistake number one. You never leave a child alone... in a bar... where anyone is able to approach them."

"Okay, you got me there. Fine. I'll text Amber first thing in the morning to make sure that she is okay with you joining our playdate."

"You mean sing-along," Lucas corrected. "There will be much singing and dancing and even some costume changes if you play your cards right."

"Good. Now that we got that settled, here, drink this. You're looking awfully thirsty standing there, watching me make your drink."

Lucas's cheeks blushed.

God, he was fucking cute when he was embarrassed.

Their fingers brushed against one another, sending a jolt of electricity through them. They both jumped, startled by the sudden burst of energy.

"You do realize that I am trying to *clean* this place. And here you are, making it dirty once again."

Caden gave him a filthy smirk that sent the tips of Lucas's ears blushing.

"Most people don't complain when I make things a little dirty."

Lucas's mouth dropped open.

He liked teasing Lucas. There was something sweet and endearing about the way his cheeks turned red, and he bashfully looked away when he was embarrassed. The guy was too fucking cute for words.

"I'm heading downstairs to get more cleaner," Lucas said over his shoulder as he carried a mop and bucket toward the back.

"Wait up! I'll join you." Caden hopped down off the bar, chasing after him with his drink.

Once they were in the basement, Lucas began opening boxes, searching for something to remove stains from metal surfaces.

"Damn it. I could have sworn I saw some cleaner here a few days ago."

"Here, let me help." Caden set down his drink and started rummaging through the boxes on the floor and the storage shelves Ace had installed a few months ago, part of his "stay organized" initiative.

When it was clear there was no cleaner in the basement, Caden got an idea.

"Hey, hold up." Caden walked over to the far wall and stopped in front of the broken lamp. He glanced over his shoulder and gave Lucas a stern look. "Don't tell anyone what you are about to see. If Marcus finds out that I showed you this, he will personally rip my nuts off. Can I trust you?"

Lucas stared at him curiously before nodding his head in agreement. "Of course. Whatever it is, it stays between you and me."

Turning back to the wall, Caden turned the fixture to the left and pulled the wall forward, revealing Marcus's hidden room of illegal toys.

Lucas gasped behind him.

"Holy shit. What is this?" he asked, stepping forward and following Caden into the secret room.

"This, here, is the *room that does not exist.*"

Lucas's eyes went wide as he took in the room around him.

"Blade, Nikolai, Ace and I run pick-up and delivery for Marcus. We transport guns, make drug runs, and even procure certain rare and hard-to-find items. This room is where we keep all the merchandise until Marcus is ready for us to make the delivery. Like I said, only a select few know about this room, so you can't tell a soul that I let you in here."

He hoped that he could trust Lucas not to blab his mouth.

Lucas walked around the room, taking a look at all the items. He seemed intrigued and curious, opening boxes and picking up guns as he browsed.

"Shit! Are those snakes?" Lucas asked, jumping away from a few tanks containing various species of the slithering reptiles.

"Yeah, we got some dude who likes to do research, so we catch these guys for him and then deliver them when he needs them," Caden explained as he began looking through some boxes on the floor.

He was pretty sure that he had seen a box of cleaner somewhere that they used to disinfect the tanks when not in use.

"Bingo!" Caden shouted, lifting the lid off one of the boxes. "Found you some extra cleaner."

Lucas walked over to where he stood, no longer interested in the cleaning products he was originally searching for. He bent down and picked up a few bottles without actually looking at what he was grabbing.

"So, how often do you guys do these jobs for Marcus?"

Caden shrugged. "A few times a month. It brings in some pretty good cash for the crew, and Marcus is making a pretty good name for himself in the criminal underworld."

"Wow, you guys are pretty gangster after all."

Laughing, Caden headed to the door. "Yeah. You should see me when I'm on muscle duty."

"Muscle duty?" Lucas asked, stopping and staring at Caden.

Caden flexed his bicep and gave Lucas a wink. "Cartels

pay extra when they hire the crew to protect their asses during high-risk meetings or deliveries."

He swore he saw Lucas's cock twitch in his pants.

Yeah, he was totally getting a boner thinking about him being all tough and manly.

Caden liked the thought of the boy getting turned on thinking about him as the protector. He wanted to explore that scenario a little bit more later on, but for now, *Mr. Broadway* had chores to get done.

"Come now. Don't you have some toilets that need scrubbing?"

Lucas gave him the finger as he walked past him and exited the room.

The boy was feisty when he wanted to be.

Caden loved it.

16

LUCAS

*T*ugging the corner of the blanket, Lucas smoothed out the edges and patted it lightly when he was done.

"There! That looks much better", Lucas said to himself, feeling pleased that everything looked perfect.

Why was he feeling so nervous? He loved *Hairspray* and loved sing-alongs. He hadn't attended one since he made his escape from Los Angeles. Back before he ran away from... *him.*

He still hated saying his name. It was as though saying it out loud might somehow alert him to his whereabouts and summon him. Like the devil materializing when you wanted to make a deal, so would his ex if he thought about him for too long.

It had been about two months since that frightening night, and Lucas was finally starting to feel as though he could breathe again. He was beginning to make friends—

well, friends with the big, scary guys at the bar. He was also starting to save some money and, perhaps, even opening his heart once more. Too bad it was for a guy who was straight, had a child, and was not interested in gay men.

Well... are you really sure about that? He did seem to enjoy that hand job you gave him a few weeks ago.

Yeah, and then he freaked out and ran away.

That morning had probably just been a moment of convenience. Caden was horny and figured, "Hey, why not let the horny gay guy jack me off?"

It happened all the time. Straight men taking advantage of a convenient blow job or hand job. And why not? They got to bust a nut and spent the rest of the day feeling like king shit, knowing that they made some gay boy's fantasy come true by feeding them their cock.

Lucas had fooled around with enough "not gay" straight men to recognize the signs.

He and a few of his friends had attended a hockey game during their first year of college, but they had no interest in watching the actual game. The five of them had scored cheap tickets and spent the game drinking beer and chatting about overly enthusiastic hockey fans.

The night was fun. He couldn't exactly remember which team won, but he really didn't care when it got down to it. Following the game, his friends had suggested stopping in at the sports pub next door to continue with their drinking fest.

So, five theater majors made their way next door and ordered a pitcher of beer—just like any heterosexual man would do. After cheersing and slamming down their mugs, they began chugging their beers and continued on with their queerfest.

It was only after about an hour that Lucas noticed a large, burly man with a neatly trimmed beard wearing a ball cap, staring at him from across the bar.

At first, Lucas was convinced that the man was staring at someone else, but when the man grabbed his crotch and then nodded toward the back door, Lucas finally made the connection.

He made up an excuse, then slipped out back, hoping to run into the sports-cap-wearing beast of a man.

"Took you long enough," a rough voice said from the shadows. The man stepped forward, his face barely visible in the dim light cast from the bar. "Been tryin' to get your attention all night."

"Well, here I am," Lucas responded, nervous as ever.

He had never really hooked up with a random guy before, especially out in the back of a bar. It was both exciting and terrifying at the same time.

"Just so you know, I'm straight. I don't kiss. I don't suck cock, but I'll let you get down on your knees and blow me."

It was clear to Lucas that this was going to be all one-sided. The big burly dude was going to get to bust his load while Lucas would remain untouched and do all the work.

He hoped that the man's dick would be worth the effort.

"Sure thing," Lucas said, sinking down to his knees.

Perhaps, one day, a hot, aggressive man will want to return the favor to him.

At least he had his fantasies.

"Lucas!" A high-pitched squeal rang out, startling Lucas from his thoughts and scaring half the birds that had been drinking water from a fountain in the park.

Lucas stood, smiling.

"Lizzy!" Lucas greeted, spreading his arms and letting the little girl barrel into his chest. "How's it going, my little peanut?"

"Sooo good! Mommy said that I could watch the funny movie with you and Daddy. And then Daddy bought us some gummies and sour candies and even candy bracelets!" she screamed, holding up her arm to show off her latest piece of jewelry.

Lucas looked up at Caden, who was carrying his own blanket and what looked like a daddy's bag of children's treats.

"Looks like Daddy got you all the essentials," Lucas noted, giving Cade a wink. "You're going to need all that sugar to give you lots of energy to keep dancing with Daddy and me!"

"Haha. Fat chance. This butt don't move like that," Caden added, giving his butt a little shake.

Lizzy laughed and clasped her hands over her mouth.

"Oh, I'm sure it's got some awesome moves," Lucas noted, his cheeks quickly turning a mild shade of pink.

Caden opened his mouth but quickly closed it again, seeming to decide against voicing whatever dirty comment had surely just sprung to mind in that mischievous head of his.

They both stared at each other as Caden fought his inner

devil. It appeared that *Daddy Caden* had rules when it came to acting appropriately around his daughter.

Seeing this side of Cade was extremely sexy. *Fuck, he was a goner.*

The butterflies fluttering in Lucas's stomach were in full party mode. Damn, he hadn't felt this nervous about a hangout since he was a teenager going on his first date with a boy.

Relax. You're just watching a sing-along with a dude and his little girl. This is not a date. He didn't ask you out, don't forget.

No, but he did insist that he join them today. He wasn't subtle about it either. What straight man insists on having another dude come and watch a musical with him and his daughter? None.

Caden laid out the second blanket he was carrying and organized himself nice and close to where Lucas was sitting.

The park was starting to fill up—mostly parents with small children and a few curious people who happened to be passing by on their afternoon walk.

A large movie screen and two huge speakers had been set up along the far side of the park, optimizing as much of the space as possible for viewers and patrons selling candy and snacks.

"Hey! Is that?" Lucas asked, pointing at the man connecting the speakers to some additional equipment.

"Yeah, that's Marcus. He loans out his speakers to the library for these movie nights and sing-alongs."

Lucas's head snapped in Caden's direction.

"You mean you knew about this event already?"

Caden shrugged. "Yeah, he's been helping out with the event for years. We also do barbecues, toy drives, and even a storytime with Santa, come Christmas. You should see Ace when he's dressed in his little elf costume. Talk about a feisty little twink." Caden leaned back on his hands as they chatted.

"Why didn't you say something the other night?"

"Oh. I wasn't planning on coming to this event. Sing-alongs are not really my thing." He straightened up, then leaned in close so that his daughter couldn't hear. "I do have balls, you know."

Lucas turned and shook his head. So much toxic masculinity. It was both annoying and a turn-on.

Sometimes, Lucas wondered if he might be fucked in the head.

"And one day, your balls will be big enough to do this!" Lucas stood and reached into a bag he had propped at the side of his blanket. "Hey, Lizzy, how do you feel about dressing up and helping me show your dad how this song is supposed to be sung?"

Lizzy's eyes went wide as she spotted the large blue wig Lucas was holding out to her.

"Yes!!" she shrieked, tearing the wig from Lucas's hand and throwing it onto her head lopsided.

Caden laughed.

"Here, let me help." Lucas straightened out the wig he had happened to find at a thrift shop a few days earlier.

Once she was all fixed and fastened correctly, Lucas pulled out his own bright-pink beehive wig he had found, thankfully, this morning, at the same shop. When he decided to join Cade and his daughter, he ran to the shop early in the morning, hoping to buy another wig. Miraculously, he found the sucker stashed behind a top hat and a Jason hockey mask.

"I like your wig," a little girl said next to them as she struggled with a thin scarf her mom was trying to fasten to her head.

"Would you like some help, ma'am?" Lucas asked, walking over to the woman sitting next to them.

"Oh, that would be lovely. I've seen this once in a movie, but I don't know how to make it stay up."

Lucas smiled. He grabbed three bobby pins from his magic bag—because you must always come prepared—and began maneuvering the scarf around the little girl's hair.

Once he had finished helping the little girl, he glanced at Cade, who was leaning back on his elbows and smiling up at him.

God, the man looked stunning. He wore a tight white shirt under a checkered button-up that hung open loosely at his sides. In addition, he wore a pair of tight blue jeans that hugged his thick thighs and seemed to cradle his bulge as if the material were trying to snuggle up against his junk.

It wasn't that long ago that Lucas had been cradling that junk as well. Talk about a fantasy come true.

"Care to join us?" Lucas asked, reaching out toward the hunky piece of man-bait.

A pair of bright-blue sapphires stared back at him, looking entertained.

"Nah, I think I'll sit out the opening number. See how you professionals do it."

"Yeah, it's probably best that you watch Lizzy and me first. We wouldn't want you to pull a hip."

Lizzy giggled as she took Lucas's hand. "Come, let's go dance by the screen!"

The next thing Lucas knew, he was being pulled through a maze of blankets and bodies, collecting children and kidnapped parents as he and Lizzy made their way down to the front.

Once they reached their destination, a crowd of screaming kiddies and dancers unleashed havoc on the park, rocking and laughing and screaming.

Lucas loved it.

Glancing back over his shoulder, he couldn't help but notice the huge smile plastered on Caden's face as he watched the chaos—or should he say "kiddy talent show"—begin.

17

CADEN

*W*atching Lucas interact with Lizzy was the cutest thing in the world. Lizzy had really taken a shine to Lucas, mimicking his every dance move and doing her best to sing along with the characters on-screen.

They had seen the movie once before, but Caden doubted if Lizzy remembered much of it. She had spent so much of the movie asking who each character was and why they had such funny-looking hair and outfits. Try explaining to a six-year-old about the evolution of fashion and hairstyles.

It was around the first twenty-minute mark of the movie when Lucas sent Lizzy to retrieve her daddy and convince him that it was her Christmas wish that her daddy would dance with her like the other girls and boys in the movie.

Lucas, the conniving little...

The man just smirked when Caden joined him and the collection of children, who were now all dancing and screaming like a bunch of hopped-up kittens having their first taste of catnip.

At some point during the movie, Caden convinced the dancing devils to take a break and join him back on the blanket for some popcorn and sodas.

"Can we have candy too?" Lizzy's eyes lit up at the thought of all that sugar just waiting to be ingested.

Caden felt a bit guilty returning his daughter to her mom, all hopped up on sugar—a.k.a kiddie crack. But hey, he was the fun dad. Lizzy could stay up a little later, telling her mother about how much fun she had with her amazingly cool dad.

Once the movie was over, Cade waited in the parking lot for Lizzy's mother to pick her up. She was coming from a date with a new guy she was seeing, so she offered to swing by the park and grab their daughter on her way back.

Lucas sat on a bench a few feet away, hoping to go unnoticed by Caden's ex and the woman who had given birth to Lizzy. Caden didn't resist. He understood the importance of giving people their space and private moments with family.

He wondered if Lucas had any family. He never mentioned any siblings or parents.

"Mommy!" Lizzy screamed as her mother pulled into the lot, driving a beat-up minivan.

The van was at least fifteen years old and had belonged to Amber's neighbor before he sold it to Lizzy's mom six years ago.

Caden took his daughter's hand and led her to her mom's van. He popped open the side door and helped his little princess into the seat. He fastened her seatbelt and made sure that the strap was nice and snug.

"Did you have a good time?" Amber asked her daughter with a huge smile.

Caden was grateful that he and Amber were still great friends. Sharing a child would have been so much harder if they hated each other. They had tried to date on and off after Lizzy was first born, but it became clear pretty quickly that they were not compatible as a couple in any way.

He didn't regret any of it. He loved Lizzy and respected Amber, but they were just not right for each other in the end.

"Yeah, I had a great time with Daddy and Lucas!"

"Lucas?" Amber asked, flicking a glance in Caden's direction, clearly forgetting the conversation they had earlier in the day.

"Yeah, he's one of the new guys at work I was telling you about. The one who suggested this thing."

And he gives fantastic hand jobs.

"Oh yeah." She nodded, turning her attention back to her daughter in the rearview mirror. "Are you ready to go? Say goodbye to Daddy, sweetheart."

Lizzy blew her daddy a kiss and turned her attention back to the blue wig that Lucas had insisted she keep.

"You never know when the mood might strike, and you'll want to put on a performance with Daddy!" Lucas had informed his daughter.

Caden considered those threats of terror.

As Caden watched Amber drive away with the only

thing that gave his life meaning, he turned his attention back to the handsome man sitting patiently on a bench, waiting for him.

"You got any plans for the rest of the night?" Caden asked, giving the boy a hopeful smile.

The corners of Lucas's lips turned upward.

"No. What did you have in mind?"

"Picnic under the stars?" Caden asked, hoping that his suggestion wasn't too forward.

"Sounds romantic."

"That's me. Mr. Romance. Don't tell anyone. I have a bad-boy image to maintain."

Chuckling, Lucas picked up his items and followed Caden out of the parking lot.

Caden stopped to grab them some burgers, fries, and cold salads to eat under the stars. He even ran into a corner store to grab a bottle of wine and some beers for them to enjoy.

"You sure you don't want any money?" Lucas asked for the twentieth time that evening.

"No. When a man invites someone out for a 'romantic picnic,' as you so eloquently put it, he pays for dinner and any expenses incurred as part of that night."

"You're very confusing, you know," Lucas responded, giving him a sideways glance.

"What do you mean?" Caden asked, unsure what he was inferring.

"This. Here. If it were a date, I'd be impressed as hell. But considering your reaction the last time we 'hung out,' I'm not really sure what this is supposed to all mean," he said, holding up the bag of food and supplies.

Caden's cheeks flushed. He still felt horrible for the way he reacted. Lucas didn't deserve that kind of reaction and then to be ignored for two weeks after that.

That shit was all on him.

"Where are we going anyway?" Lucas asked, turning around and glancing in all directions.

"The funny thing is that the best place to stargaze just so happens to be on Old Man Benson's farm."

Seeing Lucas's reaction was priceless. His mouth fell open, and his eyebrows scrunched together.

"So you invited me out on a romantic date at my own house?"

Caden couldn't help but chuckle. "Romantic as fuck, isn't it?"

They walked up Old Man Benson's dirt driveway and looped around to the back of his barn.

"This is the perfect spot right here," Caden said as he set the food down and began unfolding the blankets and laying them down on the field.

Once they were all settled, Caden popped the cork on the bottle of wine that he had purchased and began filling their plastic cups.

"To getting to know one another and being romantic as fuck," Caden toasted, clacking his cup against Lucas's.

Lucas rolled his eyes. "Still confusing as fuck."

Caden passed him a burger and some cold salads before he began digging in himself. It wasn't fancy, but it was him.

Over the next few hours, they talked about their friends and family.

Lucas had one older sister who lived on the East Coast. They weren't close, and he had left her a message that he was going to be traveling through Europe for the next few months when he decided to leave his ex and LA. He figured that he would contact her again once all the heat had died down and he was able to safely get in touch.

His parents? Well, they were useless, according to Luc. They had taken off to South America to pursue their dream careers studying endangered species—something Lucas had absolutely no interest in. He spoke to them once in a blue moon, but in his eyes, he had no parents.

Lucas still avoided talking about his ex, only stating that he was a horrible man and that it took him a lot to gather the courage to leave him.

Sensing the boy's failing mood, Caden decided to steer his attention toward the stars above. The night was warm, and the sky was clear, perfect for gazing up at the heavens.

"I can't believe how many you can see," Lucas marveled, lying on his back, arm tucked under his head. His chest rose and fell as he breathed in the warm summer night.

Caden lay beside him, their shoulders touching ever so slightly. He felt calm and connected. Like somehow, all of his stress and worries had been cut in half. Like somehow, Lucas had accepted the burden and sucked his troubles out of him through his body. It was strange, but being around the boy always made him feel relaxed and at peace.

That was, of course, when he wasn't freaking out and running off like a scared pansy-ass.

Still, being under the night sky with Lucas somehow felt right.

Feeling at peace, Caden stared up at the stars and let himself just be in the moment.

"I used to sneak over here when I was in high school. I'd lie down on the grass, stare up at the stars, and wonder how many planets had aliens on them."

"That movie always scared me."

"What? *Aliens*?" Caden asked, turning his head ever so slightly.

"Yeah, the one with Sigourney Weaver. The woman was badass in it, but the way those aliens moved and were able to hide in any dark corner always scared the shit out of me."

Heart pounding in his chest, Caden slowly slid his hand until it was barely touching Lucas's.

He felt the boy's body tense.

Swallowing hard, Caden slid his hand over Lucas's and gently took his hand in his.

Caden held his breath while he waited for Lucas to say something. Gradually, he felt Lucas's warm fingers begin to curl around his.

The beating of his heart quickened.

Why was he so nervous? He wasn't a virgin, and he had held hands with people before.

Women. He'd held hands with women. That was the huge distinction.

Yet holding Lucas's hand in his was not the same. There was more to it. More feeling than he had ever felt before.

Cade's heart continued to beat against his chest.

"Cade?" Lucas's voice was soft and cracked slightly when he pronounced the D.

"Yeah?" Cade managed to choke out. His heart was racing as he waited for Lucas's question.

"What are we doing here?"

The question was so innocent.

And to be honest, Caden wasn't quite sure himself. All he knew was that when Lucas mentioned his fear, he wanted to take his hand and comfort him.

"I... I'm not sure."

"Are you bi?" Lucas's voice was barely a whisper. He sounded so nervous, and there was a slight tremor in his voice.

"No. I don't think so." There was a long pause as Caden stared up at the night sky.

The stars above them twinkled as their breathing grew more in sync. Their hands remained connected as they quietly listened to the crickets sing in the fields around them.

Caden took a breath, then slowly added, "I... I've never been attracted to guys before. But for some reason, I like being around you. I feel good when you smile. I want to hold your hand when you need someone to comfort you. I like listening to you talk and love watching you sing while you clean. Being around you makes me feel calm, like all of my troubles are somehow less important when I'm with you."

Caden stared up at the stars and wondered how many aliens were watching them right now. "I want to be the one to protect you, be there when you need someone to hold you."

He felt Lucas squeeze his hand.

Caden sat up on one elbow and looked down at Lucas's moonlit face. His chestnut eyes reflected the stars, and the light from the moon cast a perfect silhouette across the young man's face.

"I loved seeing you with Lizzy today. You have such a great spirit and are so kind to those around you." Caden traced the contours of Lucas's face with his fingers. His heart was pounding, and all he wanted to do was kiss the man.

Eyes locked together, Caden leaned in and gently brushed his lips against Lucas's. His lips were soft and warm and tasted like red wine. He felt Lucas's breath against his lips and wondered why it had taken him this long to taste those gorgeous lips.

Mouth opening slightly, Caden welcomed Lucas's tongue inside as the boy wrapped an arm around Caden's shoulders and pulled him closer.

Melting into each other, they shared an undeniable instant connection.

Lucas gave a moan as he tilted his head slightly, exploring more of Caden's mouth and lips. They teased each other, kissing and licking and gently caressing one another's faces as they went.

The world around them fell away as Caden lost himself in the magic of Lucas's lips.

Every moan, every hitch of Lucas's breath, had Caden's dick thickening until it got to the point where he was pretty damn sure his cock was going to burst through his zipper.

"Inside. Now," Caden gasped.

"What?" Lucas chuckled, his lips still firmly pressed against his.

"Inside. House. Naked. Bed." The words fell from Caden's mouth in between desperate kisses and gasps for air.

His dick was suddenly in control.

Caden grabbed Lucas by the hand and yanked him to his feet.

Chuckling, they both ran toward the double set of barn doors like two horny newlyweds on their wedding night.

"Upstairs, now!" Caden huffed, pulling the door closed behind them as he pushed Lucas toward the loft and, hopefully, his waiting bed.

His heart was pounding as he rushed up the ladder and stepped into Lucas's bedroom/living area. He hadn't been in this space since the morning of the "incident" and was both eager and terrified at the same time.

Part of him was beyond excited to be doing this, finally getting Lucas alone and naked once more. Another teeny, tiny part of him worried that he might lose his nerve and run off once again. He hoped that wouldn't happen. He really wanted to do this and didn't think Lucas would forgive him if he had another freak-out.

Gasping, they both fell onto the bed, a jumbled pile of limbs and way too much clothing.

"You sure?" Lucas asked, stopping momentarily once he tore off his shirt.

"Fuck yes," Caden growled, tossing his own shirt across the room and fumbling with his belt next.

He was desperate. He needed to be naked and holding Lucas's warm body up against his.

"Why are those still on?" Caden asked, staring down at Lucas's underwear and laughing.

The boy looked wrecked. His eyes were dilated, and his chest was heaving. His bottom lip was being pierced between his teeth as he stared hungrily up at Caden.

Caden reached down and tore off Lucas's underwear. Yes, there was no finesse or romance. Just pure animalistic need.

He'd never felt so horny and needed to see Lucas naked immediately.

Lucas's cock bounced against his abdomen once it was freed from its constraints.

"On your back," Lucas demanded. "I want to taste that cock of yours."

Staring down at the boy, Caden gave him a snarl, then flipped onto his back. He liked this bossy side of Luc. It was both assertive and forceful, not like the bashful busboy he had met only a few months ago.

"Have at it," Caden said, holding his dick up from the base and watching as Lucas leaned down and aligned his lips with his raging-hard mushroom head. He knew that Lucas liked his men bossy, controlling, and somewhat pigs in bed.

If he wanted a dirty horny biker dude, the boy was going to get one.

Cade's body was buzzing with excitement. He'd never been this turned-on by someone. He couldn't wait to feel the boy's mouth stretched around his cock and sliding up and down the full length of his shaft.

He didn't have to wait long.

Without warning, Lucas swallowed Caden's cock right down to the base. The hunger. The desperation. All of it was so fucking hot.

"Holy fuck!" Caden shouted, caught off guard by the boy's sudden attack on his cock and mad deep-throating skills.

Caden wasn't small by any means, and most women had to warm up to swallowing his dick all the way down to the base, but this man. This man right here was a fucking pro!

Rubbing Caden's balls in one hand while holding the base of his cock with the other, Lucas began his assault on Caden's dick and his heterosexual image.

Moaning, slurping, and licking, Lucas swallowed it all without gagging or complaining.

They say some people were born to suck dick. Lucas was born to swallow it.

The boy had skills.

"Jesus, you keep that up, and I'm going to come," Caden huffed out in between gasps of breath and gripping the sheets. He wasn't sure where to put his hands and wanted to last longer than four minutes.

"Then come."

"No. I want to try sucking on yours first," Caden heard himself say. He was kind of surprised that he had admitted it out loud, but he would be lying if he said that the thought hadn't crossed his mind at some point over the last few weeks.

Lucas popped his head up and stared into Caden's heated eyes.

"You sure? Cause I don't need you to suck my dick if you don't want to."

Was the guy worried that he would run away screaming? Or perhaps that he would be terrible at sucking dick?

"I want to. Please."

Lucas's lips pulled back in an evil grin. That was all the boy needed to hear, apparently.

He slid out from between Caden's hairy thighs and lay down on the bed in his original position.

"Let me know if I'm doing it wrong or if I do something that you don't like."

"I will. Trust me, with your mouth on my dick, you will never be able to do anything wrong." Lucas chuckled, playing with the light-brown beard that covered Caden's face.

That was another thing that Caden had come to learn about Lucas. Apparently, he loved men with facial hair.

Gripping the base of Lucas's cock, Cade stared down at the angry hard shaft, wondering what a cock would taste like? Would it be all warm and salty? Would it have no taste at all?

Most women seemed to love sucking his dick, so he assumed that his own cock must have a great taste.

But what if he sucked at sucking dick?

Would Lucas have the heart to tell him to stop?

Would Lucas coach him through it and give him pointers like they were playing a game of rugby?

No man ever wants to hear that they are bad in bed. But what did he have to compare it to? Eating a girl's pussy was not like sucking a man's dick. Both skills were very different and required different levels of skill sets.

But what man ever did not enjoy having his dick sucked? Even when a woman was terrible, he still loved having her mouth around his dick and busting a nut. Was it the same for gay men?

Caden had never felt so vulnerable or insecure in his life.

"Stop getting inside your head. Start off by licking the tip of my cock. Then, if you feel more confident, you can try licking the sides of my shaft. You don't need to be a hero and shove the whole thing into your mouth right away," Lucas joked.

He appreciated the guidance but still stared at the throbbing hard cock only inches from his face. This was also the closest his mouth had ever been to another man's penis—well, to any penis.

"Perhaps I should have started with someone a bit smaller." Caden grimaced as Lucas slapped his hand.

"You never talk about sucking another man's dick when you are about to go down on them. As far as you're concerned, my dick is the only dick in this whole godforsaken world."

Was that jealousy he detected in Lucas's voice?

Caden smirked. He kind of liked seeing this jealous, possessive side of Lucas.

"Your dick is the only dick that I want in my mouth." Caden decided to reassure him. It wasn't a lie. Caden had zero desire to get intimate with or even suck on another man's dick. His eyes and his desires were only for the boy lying beneath him.

With that last thought, Caden dove down and swallowed Lucas's dick.

No point in wasting time.

Lucas let out a gasp, most likely surprised by Caden's jump to step number three. Caden was never one to shy away from a challenge or deny himself something that he wanted. He knew the boy's dick would end up in his mouth eventually, so why waste any time procrastinating?

He closed his eyes and let the realization that he had a man's dick in his mouth slowly roll over his consciousness.

This was it. He could do this.

Using his tongue, he began to massage the underside of Lucas's cock. He felt the shaft thicken.

Fuck, that was hot.

He had done that. Lucas's cock was getting harder because of him.

Caden felt exhilarated.

Holding the base firmly in place, Caden began moving his mouth up and down the shaft.

A moan escaped Lucas's lips.

He had caused that.

Caden felt his own cock thicken. *Fuck, this was so hot.*

Breathing through his nose, Caden continued sucking.

"Fuck that feels good." Lucas moaned, running his fingers through Caden's hair as he worked his dick between Caden's lips.

"Is that alright?" Caden asked, quickly lifting his mouth and hoping for some validation.

"Relax and open your throat. It helps with taking a cock deeper and minimizes the gagging reflex. But other than that, you're doing amazing, stud." Lucas smiled, continuing to play with Caden's facial hair.

Receiving such praise made the butterflies in Caden's stomach do flips on their own.

He needed more. He needed to kiss Lucas's lips.

Without warning, he popped off Lucas's dick, then slid his large body on top of the boy, pinning him to the bed as he searched for Lucas's mouth.

With his full weight on top of Lucas, Caden's hands clawed at Lucas's sides, grabbing hold of his ass as he gave it a hard squeeze.

He was desperate. He was horny. He was so fucking turned-on.

The boy's body tensed. He went still and cold for a moment before he began pounding his fists against Caden's chest.

What the fuck? Was this part of the foreplay?

"No. NO!" Lucas screamed, pounding hard against his body.

Below him, Lucas's eyes were shut tight as he continued to fight against Caden's thick body.

"Luc—" Caden began before he realized that the boy was panicking.

He quickly jumped off Lucas, falling off the bed and hitting his head hard against the nightstand.

"Ow," Caden groaned, struggling to sit up while rubbing the sore spot at the back of his head. "Lucas, are you—" His voice cut off.

Lucas was lying on the bed, curled up on his side, sobbing.

What the hell just happened? Did he hurt the guy?

Cautiously, he reached up onto the bed and gently touched Lucas's bare shoulder. The boy flinched, then continued sobbing.

Slowly, Caden got up from the floor and settled down on the bed next to Lucas.

"Hey, what's going on, babe?" He wasn't sure what had happened. One minute they were going at it like bunnies in heat, then the next, Lucas was freaking out like he was being attacked.

Attacked.

Attacked!

Had he...?

"I'm sorry if I scared you," Caden said softly, gently caressing the boy's shoulder, trying to offer him some comfort. He wasn't exactly sure what the boy needed or how best to comfort the man.

Shaking his head, Lucas peered up at him through tear-stained lids.

"I-I'm sorry. Having your body suddenly on top of mine like that gave me flashbacks of my ex. I... I'm sorry. I didn't mean to freak out on you like that." He covered his face with his hands and continued to sob.

Caden's heart sank. He never wanted to see Lucas in pain or agony, and knowing that he was the cause of such a traumatic experience, made him feel like the biggest asshole in the world.

"Shhh, none of that. You never need to apologize to me. I'm sorry for not being more sensitive to your needs. I was caught up in the moment and didn't think that perhaps someone who escaped an abusive relationship might have a few triggers when being intimate in the bedroom."

Lucas just lay there, hands still covering his face. Shivering.

Caden reached for the covers and gently pulled them up over the boy's body. Lucas welcomed them, folding himself further into the blanket and letting out a gentle sigh.

"I'm going to run downstairs and get you some water. Do you want me to grab anything else for you?"

Lucas shook his head.

Nodding, Caden grabbed his underwear off the floor and made his way down the ladder to the makeshift kitchen below. He grabbed two bottles of water and then bounded back up the ladder once again.

"Here, take a few sips. It might help you feel better."

Lucas reached for the bottle and did as he was told.

"Do you want me to leave?" Caden asked, still unsure what he needed or wanted. He had never dealt with anyone who had escaped an abusive relationship before.

"No. Stay. Can you come cuddle up against me?" Lucas asked, lifting the back of the blanket.

"Of course I can. You let me know what you need, babe."

Sliding in behind Lucas, he let the boy guide his arms into a position that he was comfortable with.

"I'm sorry again if I ruined your night," Lucas whispered, arms wrapped tightly around Caden's.

"You didn't ruin anything. This is still the best date I have ever had. And now, I get to cuddle up against the sexiest man I've ever met."

Lucas chuckled. "God, I'm a mess."

Caden squeezed his body gently.

"No, you're not. You had something horrible happen to you, and now your body just needs some time to adjust. You just let me know what I can do to help or what you need from me."

"This. Just being patient and holding me close like this helps. I think the fact that you were on top of me and I suddenly felt trapped is what scared me. In this position, I can still escape from the front if I need to."

Caden kissed the back of Lucas's neck lightly.

"Whatever you need, babe. I'll always have your back."

Lying close, Caden listened to their hearts beat together.

While he might not have busted a load, this, right here, was so much more fulfilling.

He nestled in closer to the boy, enjoying the feel of his body snuggled up against his.

Caden breathed in his scent as he listened to the steady rhythm of his calming heart.

He would be whatever the boy needed. Whenever he needed it. The boy was his to protect. His to care for. His to grow to...

Slowly, his lids closed, and sleep overcame him.

18

LUCAS

*T*here was something warm and safe about being wrapped in Caden's arms. They were firm yet gentle. Like he was trying to protect him but also make him feel safe and able to escape if needed.

Opening his eyes slowly, Lucas stared out into the darkness before him.

The room was quiet, except for the soft breathing coming from behind him. At some point, they had fallen asleep spooning with Caden's arms wrapped firmly around his body.

Remembering the way he had reacted last night made Lucas's stomach turn. It wasn't that he was afraid of Caden or worried that he might hurt him because he knew that he never would.

It was the way Caden's body suddenly pinned him down on the bed. His full weight on top of him as he struggled to find his lips to kiss.

That force.

That aggression that he had once found such a turn-on was suddenly betraying him.

It all happened so fast.

A quick flash of Darryl's face, giving him that evil grin as he forced himself onto him and took whatever it was that he wanted.

With Darryl, it had always been about the control. They didn't make love; they fucked with a goal of reaching *his* pleasure. His orgasm could only seem to be reached if there was a hint of terror and forced control with his partner.

It had taken Lucas about a month from when they first started dating to discover Darryl's particular taste. He wasn't looking for a partner or an equal; he was looking for someone he could control and who would service him.

By the time Lucas had realized the terrifying truth, it was too late. Darryl had his claws into him, and it was becoming more and more difficult to leave the further they got in their relationship.

Would he always fear having an aggressive man on top of him? Perhaps. But he hoped that in time and with a lot of patience, he might be able to work through his past trauma and find a way to cope with the terrifying memories.

Lying in bed with Caden's arms wrapped around him, he had never felt so safe. These were the arms of someone who cared. Someone who could be trusted. He didn't need to fear these arms. This man was good. This man was safe.

Behind him, Caden's chest rose and fell against his body,

making Lucas feel incredibly connected. It was as if they were sharing a moment in time that belonged only to them.

His heart expanded in his chest.

Fuck, he was really starting to fall for this man.

Then his bladder began to complain.

Why did one always have to take a piss right when they were comfortable and warm and never wanting to leave the spot that they were in? It was one of God's cruel jokes, sent to man to remind them that they were under his mercy. His design.

Groaning, Lucas carefully slid out of Caden's arms and slipped on his underwear. He still felt awkward walking around the house—or barn, in his case—butt-ass naked. He knew it was his place, and he should feel comfortable doing as he liked in the privacy of his own... *barn*, but it felt kind of awkward having his dick swinging around where horses used to eat and shit. Strange, but true.

He descended the ladder and headed to the bathroom.

After taking a piss, then deciding to brush his teeth and fix his hair, he reached for the bathroom door and turned the knob.

The damn thing didn't turn.

What the?

He double-checked that the door was unlocked, then tried the knob once again. It still wouldn't turn.

Oh great. He could see it now. He would either spend the rest of the night trapped in the bathroom, waiting for Caden to wake up and rescue him, or he would call out, waking the poor man and asking him to come to his rescue. Both scenarios would result in his utter humiliation.

He tried once more, pulling and twisting and cursing every god he could think of.

Then he froze.

A tiny bit of smoke began slipping in under the door.

Was there a... fire?

More smoke began to quickly seep through the gaps around the door.

Fuck!

Lucas began to cough.

The bathroom only had a small window just above the toilet that latched open, but it was nowhere near large enough for him to squeeze through.

Shit! Caden!

He had almost forgotten about the sleeping hunky man currently nestled in the comfort of his sheets.

"Caden! Fire!" Lucas screamed, hoping that his voice would be heard in the loft above the bathroom.

The bathroom was beginning to fill with smoke.

Panicking, he reached for a hand towel and quickly ran it under water. He placed the cloth over his mouth and nose and ran to open the bathroom window. At least that would let out some of the smoke.

Fear continued to flood in.

How was he going to escape? How was he going to get to Caden? Was this how his life came to an end? Burned alive in a barn death trap?

He needed to escape. He needed to save Caden.

Lucas reached for the doorknob once again and let out a yelp. The surface was scorching hot.

Shit! This was getting serious.

He began pounding on the door and screaming for Caden to wake up.

There was no way that he and Caden were going to die tonight in a fire.

What if Cade had passed out from the smoke? What if his bedroom was already on fire and Caden was being burned alive?

He needed to get out and rescue Cade. This was not how their story ended!

"Cade! Wake up! Fire!"

"Luc?" Caden's muffled voice cried from somewhere behind the door. Coughing followed.

"Cade! I'm in here! The door's stuck!"

A large thud against the door startled Lucas.

He took a step back, scared that perhaps Caden had passed out behind the door.

"Luc! Move away from the door!" Caden shouted.

Lucas took another step back.

The door trembled with each powerful bang against it. Eventually, the wood began to crack, and finally, the sharp edge of a silver axe sliced through the door, sending columns of smoke pouring in.

"Luc! This way!" Caden shouted as he pushed aside the broken planks of wood from the door and cleared a path for Lucas's escape. "Give me your hand."

Caden grabbed Lucas's hand and scooped him up and

over his shoulder, carrying him fireman-style out of the bathroom and past the blazing inferno that was quickly consuming the loft and the hallway to the bathroom.

The rescue was both terrifying and a major turn-on.

Clinging to the broad shoulders of the man carrying him as if he weighed nothing was like every wet dream he had had since his balls descended.

Watching the fire around them destroy everything in its path was horrifying.

"It's okay, I've got you," Caden huffed out in the most reassuring voice he had ever heard.

Clinging to his hero's naked torso, Lucas felt relief as they exited the barn.

Once they were clear and safe, Caden placed Lucas back on the ground. They turned and watched in horror as the barn before them was consumed by the fiery blaze.

The fire was large, and the heat was intense.

"You... you saved my life," Lucas said, wrapping his arms around Caden's neck and burying his face into his chiseled chest.

"It was your shouting that woke me up. Guess you saved mine as well," Caden said, holding him tight in a hug.

"What the hell happened?" Lucas asked as he pulled away, watching his home and the last of his possessions vanish in a ball of fire.

"No idea," Caden whispered.

The sound of a fire engine began to screech off in the distance.

"Fire's on its way. You boys okay?" Old Man Benson asked as he came running from inside his home. "What the hell happened?"

Both men just shook their heads.

They had no fucking idea.

19

CADEN

Caden sat with his arm wrapped around Lucas's shoulders. Someone had given him a blanket to wrap himself in at some point over the past two hours. They sat together on a fallen log, watching the firemen search through the wreckage, doing what firemen do.

The sun was beginning to rise, and most people were learning about the fire in the same way that small towns always discovered things—through word of mouth.

It didn't take long before word reached Marcus and the crew. Caden hadn't been able to call the guys since his cell phone had been in the bedroom next to Lucas's when the fire began. He wasn't concerned. Everything from his phone had been backed up in the cloud, so it was just a matter of getting a new phone and downloading all of his info from there.

Technology. Got to love it.

Beside him, Lucas remained silent, staring into the charred remains of what had once been his home.

It *had* to have been an electrical malfunction. They didn't use any candles or the stove to cook dinner last night, and neither of them smoked.

Thank god Lucas had gotten up to use the bathroom. Otherwise, they both might have been killed.

Fires were a nasty piece of work.

"It's all gone," Lucas whispered, barely audible.

"It's all just material things that can easily be replaced," Caden said, trying to provide the boy with some sort of comfort.

Lucas turned and glared at him. "That's easy for you to say. You have money and credit cards and a place to sleep at night. I was just starting to get my feet back on solid ground."

Caden tightened his grip on Lucas. Lucas was right. He understood his pain. He would do everything that he could to help get the boy back on his feet.

"How are you guys doing?" Marcus asked, stepping up beside them and holding out coffees for both. Caden took his while Lucas merely shook his head.

"Thanks. We're both okay. Breathed in a bit of smoke, but not enough to warrant going to the hospital."

"Still, I'll have Dr. Higgs stop by and check on you both," Marcus stated.

Dr. Higgs was a retired physician who often treated the guys from the crew. He was discreet, didn't ask questions, and always turned a blind eye.

"Where do you want me to take you guys?" Marcus asked, looking at Caden.

"My place. Lucas is going to stay with me for the time being."

Lucas's eyes came back into focus as if he had finally been pulled from whatever trance he had been in. "What? No. I... I..."

"Don't argue. You're staying with me, and that's that." Caden put his foot down.

Lucas needed to learn how to graciously accept help instead of always thinking that he was on his own. He wasn't. He had a whole crew full of brothers and sisters who now had his back.

While he may not own a motorcycle or know how to throw a punch, he was still a part of the Shadow Vipers, whether he liked it or not.

"Fine. Thank you."

"And these are for you," Ace said, passing Lucas a bag.

Reaching in, he pulled out a pair of ripped jeans and a faded Armani T-shirt. The items looked way too big for Lucas.

"Oh, sorry. Those are for you," Marcus said, taking the outfit and passing it over to Caden.

"And these are for you," Ace added, passing Lucas a pair of neatly folded black jeans and a distressed Guess T-shirt.

"Wow, these things look nice," Lucas said, lowering the blanket and pulling the shirt over his bare shoulders.

In the rush to escape, they didn't have time to throw on any clothing.

How Marcus knew that they were both waiting outside in their underwear was anyone's guess.

Once Caden had stepped into the jeans and done up his fly, he looked at himself and immediately recognized the outfit.

"This is from that..." He let his voice trail off. Marcus gave him a nod.

About a month ago, Caden and Ace had been sent to assist a driver whose truck happened to break down on the side of the road about an hour outside of Roswell. It had been late at night, so they helped relieve the driver of some of his merchandise.

Ace, being the fashion aficionado, helped Caden determine which boxes needed to be relieved and which ones could remain in the truck with the tied-up—um, temporarily incapacitated—driver, who was waiting for a... tow truck to come and assist him.

Hmm. The clothing really was stylish, as Ace had put it.

"The fire crew said they will be here for at least a few more hours doing their assessment," Damian explained once he joined the rest of the crew.

Damian was one of the guys who worked at the bar. He didn't exactly have a job title. He basically did what he was told and helped Marcus out with... *odd jobs.*

"Okay. Shall we go?" Marcus asked, looking between Caden and Lucas.

They both nodded.

Once they arrived back at Caden's place, Caden led Lucas to the spare bedroom, thinking that the boy might want some space and perhaps some time alone to process what had just happened.

Lucas nodded and thanked him before dropping down on the bed without so much as a hug goodnight.

Poor guy. Best to give him some space.

Caden couldn't sleep. He lay down on the couch and stared up at the ceiling, thinking about how close he had come to making his little girl fatherless. First thing in the morning, he was going to call his little munchkin and tell her how much he loved her.

Letting out a breath, he froze when his stomach started to growl, reminding him that it needed food and coffee. Lots of coffee.

He threw his legs over the side of the couch and glanced at his watch.

Eight a.m.

It was as good a time as any to get up. He wasn't going to get any more sleep this morning. Plus, food. He needed food. And coffee. Yes, loads of coffee.

He made his way into the kitchen and fired up the stove. Now it was time for him to show off his skills. Caden opened the fridge and pulled out the bacon.

His stomach growled.

"Patience, my pet," Caden said to his belly as he began cooking his feast.

As the bacon came to a sizzle, he heard footsteps descending his creaky stairs.

"Mornin'," a tired and disheveled Lucas announced as he

entered the kitchen and plopped his ass down at the kitchen table. "Something smells amazing."

Carrying a mug of coffee, Caden placed the cup down in front of Lucas before heading back to the stove.

"Food will be ready in a few. Got bacon crisping up, chocolate chip and blueberry pancakes keeping warm in the oven, and some fruit salad chillin' in the fridge."

"Wow, someone's been busy. Is there anything I can do to help?"

"Can you grab the maple syrup from that cupboard over there and grab the fruit salad from the fridge?"

Lucas walked over to the cupboard and peered inside.

"Umm, Cade?"

Caden removed a few strips of bacon from the pan and looked over at Lucas.

"You got some sort of sugar addiction you've been hiding from me?"

Caden was confused for a moment before he realized what Lucas was talking about.

"Ooh! That's Lizzy's special cupboard. It's got every sugar-infused candy and cereal you can imagine in there."

Lucas pulled out two monster bags of sugar-coated candies and held them up.

"Yeah. Those Marcus and I bought while on a road trip to Vegas. There was this bulk discount store right off the Interstate that I swear was run by Willy Wonka."

Caden turned back to the stove to finish up with the bacon.

Lucas brought the items to the table and began opening the brand-new bottle of maple syrup.

"Here we go," Caden said, bringing the last of the bacon and pancakes to the table.

"Mmm, smells delicious," Lucas said, but Caden could tell that the man's energy wasn't into it.

"Hey, I know that things look dark right now, but just know that you are not alone in this. You can stay here for as long as you want, and the crew will take care of whatever you need."

Just as he finished his speech, the back door to the kitchen opened, and Marcus and Ace barged in, followed by Nikolai, Alexis, and Blade.

"Mornin' assholes," Marcus greeted, carrying in a box marked *Touch and Die*.

"What are you mofos doing here?" Caden asked, leaning back in his chair to give Marcus and Ace a fist bump since their hands were full.

"We heard there was breakfast," Alexis chirped, walking in carrying a tray filled with pastries and croissants.

"Now that your crappy clothes have been burned, it's time you started dressing like the rest of us. Hot and like a badass," Blade said, dropping a box marked *Cool Shit* on the counter next to the stove. He reached inside the box and pulled out a pair of black biker boots. "I got these from... a friend of mine when his truck broke down a few months ago. Size eleven. Never been worn. They're yours now, chico," he said, nodding at Lucas.

Next, he pulled out a black leather jacket, some sunglasses, and other junk that every hot biker needed to own.

"Also, got you a box of condoms... just in case... well, you know." Blade's cheeks flushed as he glanced between Lucas and Caden.

It appeared that the rumors had already started spreading. *Was this Blade's way of saying that he was cool with Caden and Lucas boning?*

Lucas looked around the room, confused.

"I... I don't get it. What's all this stuff for?"

Marcus walked around the table and placed his hand on the boy's shoulder.

"I told you on day one. You're part of our family now. And we help family when in need. You may have lost all your stuff in that fire, but that doesn't mean you will ever go without."

Lucas's eyes teared up. He jumped up from his chair and wrapped his arms around Marcus's thick body.

"Thank you so much," Lucas sniffled. "You don't know how much all of this means to me. Everyone coming over and making sure that we're okay. Honestly, I've never had a family like this before."

Hearing him say that broke Caden's heart. How could someone so full of life not be a priority to his family?

"When you're done slobbering all over my brother, I've got a box full of nice clothes here. It's *Sons of Anarchy* meets *Queer Eye*," Ace said, standing next to the box he placed against the wall in the kitchen. This box was labeled *Really Cool Dude Shit.*

Lucas pulled away and began to chuckle. The sound was infectious. It looked like the boy's spirits were beginning to pick up.

20

LUCAS

$\mathcal{I}$t had been a rough few days having to adjust to the thought of starting over and being pissed about losing the fifteen hundred dollars he had managed to save. He didn't have a bank account—for obvious reasons—so he had been saving all of his cash in a jar hidden in the loft. He had managed to scrape together a bit of savings, which had given him a sense of accomplishment and self-worth.

While the guys were amazing at taking care of him and giving him new clothes and other essentials, like a toothbrush and condoms, apparently, Lucas knew where all of it came from—not from his hard work and sacrifice, but from the kindness and generosity of his newfound family.

He struggled with being thankful and appreciative.

"Want to play some PlayStation?" Caden asked, bending down in his loose-fitting basketball shorts and turning on the unit.

The man stood, staring at him, waiting for an answer.

Jesus Christ.

The man was clearly not wearing any underwear, and all of his thickness was bouncing around as he moved.

"What?" Caden asked, apparently clueless to the visual assault on Lucas's eyes.

Forcing his gaze away from the dangling sausage, he stared up into Caden's baby-blue eyes and swallowed hard.

"Umm... yeah. Sure. What game are we playing?"

He tried to ignore the blood that was currently rushing down to his cock, giving him a chub and craving attention.

"*Assassin's Creed.* Love this game."

Caden sat next to Lucas on the couch and took a swig of his beer. Marcus had given them both the next two nights off so that they could recover and get things settled before coming back to work at the bar.

Caden had been great. He'd been incredibly attentive, ensuring that Lucas had everything he needed. He even picked up another burner phone for him while he was out buying a replacement for his own cell phone that was destroyed in the fire.

It had been ages since Lucas played video games, and it took him a while to figure out how to control his character and actually play the game.

Over and over, it appeared that Lucas's character had an aversion to staying alive. No matter how hard he tried, his character kept meeting horrible, untimely deaths.

"I swear, I didn't know that a character could die that way," Caden noted, referring to Lucas's player's latest on-screen death.

"What can I say? I'm unique."

They both chuckled.

"And apparently horrible at video games," Caden added.

"Hey!" Lucas shouted, dropping his controller and lunging at the mouthy ass sitting beside him.

Caden's arm came up defensively as he tried to block the flying twink currently aimed at his body.

No such luck. Lucas landed, straddling one of Caden's furry legs. He began tickling the man's ribs through his T-shirt, attempting to prove that while he may suck at playing video games, he was a master at tickles and sneak attacks.

Caden's laughter was amazing. It was a deep, guttural laugh that warmed his heart and stirred the butterflies chilling in Lucas's stomach.

They hadn't said anything about sleeping together since the night of the fire. And Lucas was starting to think that perhaps Caden was trying to forget that it had ever happened in the first place. But horsing around like this and listening to the man laugh made him think that perhaps that wasn't the case.

Diving in for another jab at Caden's ribs, Lucas was flung upward when Caden lifted his hips hard in self-defense.

Holy shit!

Lucas's eyes went wide, and his cock quickly asked what was going on?

Beneath him, it appeared that Caden was *very* happy with the little game that they were playing. The man's cock was standing at full attention, ready to impale Lucas on his next downswing.

Caden chuckled. There was no denying or hiding it. It was standing at attention and clearly demanding acknowledgment.

"Uh, sorry?" he offered, staring up at Lucas and laughing.

Lucas went in for another tickle.

"Ahh, no. Not there!" Caden screamed, grabbing Lucas by the hips and pulling him into his body.

The missile pushing up between Lucas's legs had his hormones shooting out of control.

He was so horny and so turned-on, he barely had time to register what he was doing.

Both of their mouths smashed together in a frenzy of lust and hunger. They clawed at each other's bodies while trying to inhale one another's faces. There was nothing smooth or sensual about what they were doing. Their bodies were desperate. Clinging. Grabbing. Even pulling at each other.

Lucas began grinding his hips up against Cade, groaning at the thickness of Caden's cock as it rubbed up against his.

"Fuck. Yes. Right there," Caden gasped out between breaths.

They were kissing and humping, unable to get enough of each other's body.

"More. Faster," Caden pled.

Lucas wasn't going to last much longer. Caden's hands grabbed hold of his ass cheeks and gave them a firm squeeze. Fuck, he wanted Caden's dick deep inside him, spreading his ass wide open.

"Fuck, Luc. I'm gonna come if you keep doing that."

"Come for me, baby." Lucas moaned as he dove down for one more kiss before throwing his head back as he came as well.

Their orgasms were hard and intense. Caden wrapped his arms around Lucas's body and held him close as he shot his load between them.

After three or four final pumps, Caden's body relaxed under Lucas's, and the two attempted to recapture their breaths.

"Fuck. That was hot." Lucas gasped.

"I swear, I've never had an orgasm like that before," Caden whispered, then began chuckling. "I don't think I've come in my shorts since I was a teen."

They both laughed.

"Shall we go shower, my horny beast?"

"Hey, you're the one who jumped all over my junk," Caden retaliated.

"Yeah, but you're the one who almost knocked me unconscious with that battering ram."

Leaning forward, they locked lips once again.

Lucas had never felt so alive, so wanted. This was exactly what he needed.

21

LUCAS

"Distract me," Lucas huffed out, plopping his ass down in the booth across from Ace and next to Bobby.

"Well, I got fucked by a daddy with a nine-incher last night, and Bobby thinks he might have crabs."

Lucas's horrified face snapped to his right.

Bobby rolled his eyes and let out a breath.

"The guy's exaggerating. I just mentioned that my balls were really itchy for some reason today, and it kind of burns when I pee. It's nothing. Probably just too much sun yesterday," Bobby answered, giving Ace the finger.

"You really should get that shit looked at, my friend. And, also, why is your junk out in the sun?" Lucas asked, slowly sliding a few inches away from the suspect man sitting next to him. One could never be too careful.

"I may have been out yesterday trying to even out the tan."

"Yeah, your ass really could use a bit of color," Ace added. "Nothing sexy about a pale white ass jiggling."

Lucas laughed. He was glad for the distraction. Over the past few months, they had all been getting closer as friends.

Ace was gay and didn't care who knew it. Possibly because if someone had a problem with it, his bad-ass brother —as well as the whole fucking crew—would pulverize any douchebag who had anything to say.

"So, are you going to tell me what's been going on with you and Cadey-boy?" Ace asked, picking up his mojito and taking a sip.

Lucas glanced over at Caden, who was standing at the bar, playing with a rag in his hands.

"Honestly, I don't know. We have some really nice times together, and his daughter is so effing adorable, but it's just hard to figure out if he's bi, pan, or just simply horny."

"Cade? Is that the scary bouncer dude with all the tattoos?" Bobby asked as he reached under the table to scratch his balls.

"Yup. The one and only," Lucas replied, giving his buddy a questioning look as he continued to scratch his balls.

"My guess is that he wants you bad. He cornered me when I was taking a piss and threatened to end my life if I so much as touched you," Bobby noted, placing his hands back on the table.

"What?" Lucas screeched, his voice coming off much pitchier than intended.

Bobby nodded. "Yup, that's why I left early after our second date. You're cute and all, but there's no way I'm getting my ass beat by that psycho beast just for a taste of that pretty little ass of yours."

Caden was pretty built.

Lucas's heart skipped a beat at the thought of Caden threatening Bobby with pain if he so much as touched him.

There was a fine line between being *hot possessive* and *crazy possessive*. One made Lucas's dick hard, the other required a restraining order.

His ex was the latter.

"Well, there's your answer. Have you two fucked yet? I'm guessing that's why he was with you at the barn," Ace asked, swirling his drink around in his hand.

"What?" Lucas asked, his cheeks quickly heating. "No, we have not *fucked*."

Ace raised an eyebrow.

"*Well...* I may have sucked him off, but we haven't fucked... yet." Lucas wasn't sure exactly how much he should share with his friends. Caden wasn't exactly out with whatever his sexuality might or might not be.

"That's my boy!" Ace shouted, throwing his hand up in the air and waiting for Lucas to give him a high five.

Lucas eventually met his hand in the air.

"You can't say anything though. We haven't exactly discussed what it all means and whether or not he is even into dudes. It may just have been a case of him being horny and my mouth being available."

"Oh, please. I've sucked off so much straight-men dick, I'm amazed I haven't gotten myself pregnant," Ace added before taking a sip of his drink. "It doesn't mean anything.

It's just so fucking hot to do. So tell us, is he hung like a horse? He definitely looks like he is packing some serious meat."

Lucas just shrugged his shoulders and gave Ace an innocent smirk.

"Ahh, so that's how it's gonna be," Ace shot back, the feeling of betrayal clear on his face.

"What are we talking about?" a deep voice asked from behind Lucas. Both he and Bobby jumped in their seats.

"Just how big your dick is," Ace answered like they were discussing the weather or something.

"Some say it's majestic; others call it the hip breaker," Caden answered, sitting his big meaty ass down on Lucas's lap.

Caden gave a jump, then quickly looked down at the man sitting under him.

"Jesus, warn a man first before you pop a boner in his ass."

Ace and Bobby both chuckled. Lucas simply punched Caden in the back.

"Anyone ever tell you, you weigh a fucking ton?" Lucas asked, ignoring the comment.

"It's all that muscle and dick. How do you think my back feels carrying around all this weight?"

"Oh, the struggles of the hot, hung man," Ace joked, pretending to sympathize with his horse-hung friend.

"Yes, the struggle is real," Caden noted.

"Hey! You guys got to see this," Blade said, materializing out of nowhere.

He held a tablet out in front of Lucas and Caden, who was still sitting comfortably on Lucas's quivering lap.

"What's this?" Caden asked, recognizing their bar on the screen.

Caden hit play as Lucas's stomach sank.

On the screen, a video of Lucas singing and dancing as he cleaned the bar played.

"What is this?" Lucas croaked. He watched in horror as he belted out the lyrics to one of his favorite Broadway musicals.

"It's you!" Blade announced as if Lucas couldn't recognize himself and his own private performance.

"I know it's me, but why are you playing it on your tablet?"

"It's not on my tablet; it's on YouTube. I posted it there a couple of weeks ago and look! Check out the number of views it got!"

Lucas's heart caught in his chest when he saw five hundred and twenty thousand views and no less than six hundred comments.

"Dude! The internet loves you! Some of them want to hire you for their parties and shit. One guy even said he was a producer and would love you to come audition for one of his shows. And oh! Check out this guy's comment. Apparently, he went to college with you." Blade clicked on the comments section and scrolled down to a user named "Broadwaysigz02."

Lucas recognized the handle. It belonged to one of his former classmates, a queen by the name of Clayton Ross.

The man was insufferable. He was one of those fake-ass types who only talked to people when he could get something from them. It appeared that Madame Ross now desired an audience to the tune of five hundred and twenty thousand and growing.

Then, an even more terrifying thought crossed his mind. What if *he* saw the post?

Would he be able to identify the bar? Would he be able to track him down?

"You got to take it down! Now!" Lucas shouted, shoving the tablet back in Blade's face.

Blade's smile froze in place. "What?" he asked, no doubt confused by Lucas's harsh reaction. "But they love you. You're famous."

"I don't care! Take it down. Now!" Lucas shouted once again. He shoved the tablet harder into Blade's palm, hoping that he would take the damn thing. He was now in panic mode. His mind no longer worked, and he had no idea what he was doing.

His heart was pounding, and he was starting to see spots.

Was he having a heart attack? Could your heart suddenly explode in your chest? What if he *saw? What if* he *knew?*

"But? But I don't understand. Dude, you got almost six hundred thousand views! You're a fucking legend!"

Cade grabbed the tablet from Lucas's hand and smashed it down on the table.

Startled, Lucas's vision came back into focus. He watched as Caden pulled up the video on Blade's YouTube account and hit the delete button. He then opened the file marked "videos" on the man's tablet, scrolled past all the sex and jerk-off videos Blade had recorded, and hit delete on the video containing Lucas's private performance. Next, he went to the trash folder and emptied that folder as well.

Caden then shoved the tablet back into Blade's hand.

"I suggest you delete that video from your phone or any other device or cloud you might have it saved in. If I ever see that video played or posted ever again, your head is going through that fucking wall. Is that understood?" Caden snarled.

There was such rage and anger in Caden's eyes that even Lucas was a tad afraid.

Blade stared at him, shocked and confused.

"Phone. Now!" Caden ordered, causing Blade to jump where he stood.

"Yeah. Sure. Fine." He pulled his phone from the back of his jeans and quickly deleted the video.

"If anyone asks you about that video, you say you don't know anything about it. *Comprende*?"

Blade nodded.

"Come. We're going home," Caden growled, grabbing Lucas by the hand and yanking him from the booth.

Ace, Bobby, and Blade all watched as Caden pulled them through the bar and out the back door.

Lucas's heart was beating a mile a minute, partly because of the video that had been posted and partly because of Caden's aggressive display.

He was grateful that he had someone like Cade to step in and help him through this. He was in such a panic that he wasn't able to think straight. Seeing the way the man took charge and protected him had him falling in love with him even more.

Seeing the anger and aggression toward Blade, the man who had endangered Lucas's life, was both terrifying and a huge turn-on. Like he said before, fucked in the head.

Lucas knew he was in trouble. He was attracted to strong, aggressive, and protective men—even ones who might be straight. He knew that if Caden decided not to return his love, he would end up being devastated and heartbroken.

Why had he been so stupid? Why had he gone and caught feelings for the gorgeously rough bouncer with big muscles and a monster rod between his legs?

Oh, yeah, because you are gay and a masochist, apparently.

Caden tossed Lucas his spare helmet, then helped him up onto his motorcycle—another ridiculously hot trait that the boy loved about him.

The bike was black and green and looked sporty in style. Lucas didn't know much about motorcycles, but it was the type of hypermasculine bike that fit Caden perfectly. Its surfaces were smooth and sleek and probably handled effortlessly at top speeds.

Seeing Caden sitting on his bike, wearing his black leather jacket and tight-fitting jeans, Lucas found it hard to concentrate, even when his life might be coming to an end.

If *he* had seen the video, it might be time for him to run again.

Lucas hated the thought. He didn't want to leave Caden

or Lizzy or Marcus or any of the other people he had met at Ride 'em Hard. They were his new family, and he was just starting to get to know them all.

The bike roared to life between their legs.

"Hold on to me," Caden ordered as he released the brake and steered them home.

He would hold on to Caden for as long as he could. Hopefully, he could hold on to him... forever.

22

LUCAS

*W*hen they got back to Caden's place, Lucas was still in panic mode.

Had Darryl seen the video? Did his ex know where he was? Perhaps he should grab his stuff and leave town.

What stuff? You lost it all in that fire.

The fire.

Was it even an accident?

They were still waiting to hear back from the fire marshal regarding the cause of the fire.

Stop it. Don't jump to any weird conclusions. It's a barn. The fire could have been caused by many things.

He wasn't exactly the most careful the other night. He had been drinking; he'd been distracted by Cade. He could have accidentally bumped a heater or perhaps overloaded one of the fuses, causing a spark. Who knew? There was no point in panicking about it until they got back the results of the investigation.

Now, there was this video. He shouldn't have been in such a rush to delete the damn thing. He should have checked first to see who had viewed it.

All six hundred thousand names?

Yeah, that was kind of a stupid plan. But still. If he had been able to see who viewed the video, he would have been able to confirm whether Darryl had seen it.

If he used his regular handle.

No. Darryl was smarter than that. He was a police officer with nearly twenty years under his belt. He knew how to conduct investigations and surveillance without being caught. That was one of the other reasons why he was so afraid of him. It would only take one slip, one small mistake, to lead Darryl right to him.

Should he take off again... just in case?

"Stop. I can see you getting inside your own head." Caden's voice cut through the panic beginning to take hold. He was right. He was starting to lose it.

Caden entered the room, carrying a bottle of red wine and two glasses. He sat down next to Lucas on the couch and popped the cork on the bottle.

After pouring two glasses, he slid his body behind Lucas's and pulled Lucas up against his chest.

With his arms wrapped around him, Cade rested his chin in the crook of Lucas's neck.

"Look, we don't know who saw the video. It was only up for a few weeks, and the internet is a big place. Six hundred thousand could be spread out across the world. What's the likelihood that one specific man happened to see that exact video?"

Lucas turned his head slightly.

"That asshole from college did," Lucas reminded him.

"Yeah, well, it sounds like he trolls around looking for trends so that he can steal them for himself instead of trying to be original."

During the ride home, Lucas told Caden about his connection with the mystery commentator on his viral post.

Lucas snaked his fingers in between Caden's.

It was moments like these that Lucas cherished the most —the quiet, calm connection where it was just Caden and him. The gentle caress of Caden's caring touch made Lucas feel safe and protected as if he never had to worry about anyone ever hurting him again.

"Thank you for this." Lucas's voice was barely a whisper.

"I told you that I would always be here for you. I'll always protect you and be whatever it is that you need me to be."

He loved hearing those words. If only they were the truth. They weren't a couple, and Lucas had no idea where they stood. Were they friends? Lovers? Friends who occasionally fucked? He loved the idea of having Cade by his side forever, but he wasn't ready to find out if that was something that Caden wanted as well.

Lucas hoped so, but he knew that that was something Caden had to figure out on his own.

"Right now, I need you to be my drinking buddy," Lucas said, leaning to the side and grabbing their wine glasses. The liquid had breathed long enough.

Caden chuckled. "Sure thing."

They polished off the bottle of wine in less than an hour, then moved on to a second. Lucas had to admit that wine and cuddles were the perfect solution to an overloaded mind.

It was around ten when Lucas decided to take this evening to the next level.

"How about we take this party upstairs to the bath?"

"As in, you and I naked in the tub together? Or as in, I kneel next to the tub, washing your back and feeding you grapes while you relax?"

Lucas sat up. "Well, I was originally thinking the first scenario, but I'm kind of liking the sound of the second one much more."

Caden wrapped Lucas up in a bear hug and began playfully nibbling at his neck. Lucas squealed as the evil man happened to hit every single ticklish spot he didn't know even existed.

God, the man was great at getting him out of his own mind. In the last thirty minutes, he had managed to go from "his life is coming to an end" to "they overcooked my steak." That was the sign of a true partner. Someone who could be there for you when you needed them and help walk you back from the ledge when necessary.

Laughing, Lucas was able to fight Caden off and head up the stairs, shedding clothing as he ran. Distracted, he barely remembered the panic and terror he had felt only a few hours earlier.

This was how life was supposed to be—happy, full of laughter, and carefree.

When they both reached the bath, Lucas quickly plugged the tub and turned on the water.

"Here, let me." Caden squeezed past him, placing two thick scented candles on both sides of the tub. He struck a match, then lit the wicks.

"Wow. Who knew there was a romantic side to you?" Lucas joked, trying hard not to show his heart eyes to Caden.

"Yeah, well, don't tell any of the guys. I do have balls and a reputation to keep."

Stepping in close, Lucas stuck his hand down the front of Caden's underwear and cupped the man's balls.

"Yes, you do. Two nicely trimmed pairs, eagerly waiting to get some attention."

Placing his wine glass on the white tile floor next to him, Lucas sank to his knees, pulling Caden's underwear down as he went.

An angry, thick piece of meat bobbed out of Caden's boxer briefs, nearly smacking Lucas in the eye.

"Damn. You've got such a nice, fucking dick." Lucas grabbed hold of the thing by the base and ran his tongue along the underside.

A moan escaped Caden's lips.

Reaching the tip of his dick, Lucas opened his mouth wider, then placed his lips over the head of Caden's cock. His hungry, warm mouth slid all the way down to the base, only stopping once his nose touched skin.

There were two things that Lucas enjoyed doing sexually when in bed with a man: swallowing dick and getting rammed from behind doggy style.

"Fuck, baby. Your mouth feels so fucking good." Caden moaned, gently caressing the back of Lucas's head.

"You ain't seen nothing yet. Hold on to something."

With those words of warning, Lucas swallowed Caden's cock all the way down to the base before beginning his one-man mission to drain all the cum from Caden's balls.

Slurping and gagging, Lucas went down on that cock like he had been marooned on an island with no food or drink. His only source of sustenance was the glorious load contained within Caden's balls.

"Ho... ly... fuck, dude," Caden moaned out as he lost himself in the wickedness of Lucas's mouth. It was only a few seconds before Caden gripped the back of Lucas's head and began pounding into his mouth.

Caden was, by nature, a dominant man. It didn't take Lucas long to discover this truth. Even when Lucas attempted to take control and serve Caden, somehow, Caden always found a way to regain control and take what he wanted—a quality Lucas found so fucking sexy in a man but also one that had gotten him in trouble in the past.

Lucas could feel the panic begin to rise inside him as he slowly lost control of sucking Caden's dick. It was a battle. He loved the fact that Caden was making him his bitch, but struggled against that inner voice that feared Caden would become another Darryl.

As if sensing his fears, Caden softened his grip on Lucas's head and quickly passed control of his cock back to Lucas.

God, the man was perfect.

Darryl would not have considered taking care of and

addressing Lucas's fear—in fact, he would have gotten off on it—and he most definitely would not have passed control back to his partner.

The fear that had been building quickly evaporated. Caden was not his ex. While the two might share some similar qualities, they were also very different.

Darryl got off on control and fear, while Caden enjoyed control but also cared enough about his partners to adjust to any fears their partner might be feeling. While power and control were major turn-ons for Lucas, so were respect and care.

Wanting to give the man more, Lucas popped his mouth off Caden's cock and looked up into Caden's lust-filled eyes.

"Got a condom and lube?"

Caden's eyebrows nearly hit the ceiling. "Really? Sure! Yes. One sec."

Lucas chuckled as he watched Caden's pale white ass jiggle as it ran out of the bathroom and into the bedroom across the hall. He couldn't see what was happening, only heard drawers opening and slamming shut in a frenzied rush. It was like listening to an excited virgin about to lose his virginity to the slutty head cheerleader. Not that Lucas was slutty by any means.

Well, come to think about it, how many dicks did one have to suck to be considered "slutty"? Lucas had stopped counting cocks once he passed fifty. In today's day and age, cocks were so readily available that most people didn't bat an eye when they said they'd sucked more than one hundred dicks by the time they were twenty-five.

"Got it!" Caden declared, his face beaming like Christmas morning as he appeared in the doorway holding up a strip of condoms.

"Got big plans, do ya?" Lucas laughed, wondering how many times Caden thought they were going to plow his ass.

While Lucas was twenty-four and easily able to go multiple rounds, Caden was in his early thirties. If past experience was any indication, the man had one, maybe two good rounds in him before needing a long nap and perhaps a sandwich. But good for him for being so hopeful!

Realizing that the bathroom tub was still filling with water and nearly overflowing, Lucas quickly turned it off and decided to remove the plug.

Yes, it was a waste of water, but what was water against getting an ass full of Caden-dick? Priorities man. Dick over water every time.

Taking the lube from Caden, Lucas popped the cap and added some lube to his fingers.

"You ever fucked someone in the ass before?"

"No. But I'm guessing it's just like fucking a chick doggy style."

Doggy style in the pussy or ass? Now was not the time to ask for clarification.

"Yes and no. First, you need to work open your partner, making sure that they are nice and loose before shoving your dick inside. Shove it in without prepping, and you're liable to get a punch in the face."

Lucas raised a leg, resting it on the side of the tub as he began rubbing circles around his hole.

Behind him, Caden gave a moan.

"Want to try?" Lucas asked, holding up the bottle of lube for Caden to take.

"Yes," Caden whimpered.

Taking the lube, Caden drizzled some onto his fingers.

"Now, I want you to rub your fingers around my hole, being sure to spread the lube evenly around the surface. The slicker, the better." Caden nodded before doing as instructed.

Lucas closed his eyes and basked in the pleasure of Caden's long fingers as they teased the edges of his hole. *God, he felt so good.*

"Next, I want you to take two fingers and slowly insert them into my hole. Don't worry; I occasionally use a dildo when jacking off, so my ass won't take long to stretch out."

Behind him, Caden moaned. Lucas looked over his shoulder and smirked. Caden had his eyes locked on Lucas's ass while stroking his dick with his free hand.

The hungry look in Caden's eyes told Lucas that his ass was in for a railing.

"Don't get too excited; I want that cock inside me, fucking me deep and pounding me hard."

Another moan.

After a few minutes, Lucas instructed Caden to insert a third finger. Having Caden's fingers stretching out his hole was every fantasy Lucas had come true. He moaned and guided himself down on Caden's fingers, loving the way they curled up inside him, working him open and brushing against his prostate.

"Okay, I'm ready," Lucas whispered, pulling himself off Cade's fingers and reaching for the condom.

Eyes locked with Caden's, he tore open the condom with his teeth, then placed the rubber on the tip of Caden's cock. Caden's mushroom head was slightly bigger than the circumference of the condom.

Of course the man's dick was going to be bigger than the average man's.

Smirking, Caden waited with his hands on his hips for Lucas to suit him up.

"Need a hand there, bud?" the cocky asshole asked, giving Lucas a smug grin.

"You're not the first big dick I've had in my life, stud," Lucas answered, loving the jealous growl that escaped the man before him.

Stretching the latex around the head of Caden's dick, Lucas rolled the condom down the length of his shaft. He drizzled some more lube on the tip of his cock and used his hand to even it out.

"Sit," Lucas ordered, pointing to the toilet, whose lid had already been lowered.

Caden sat quickly, spreading his legs apart as he made himself comfortable.

Licking his lips, Lucas climbed onto Caden's lap and grabbed the base of his dick behind him.

"Now, I'm going to lower myself down onto your dick. You'll have to go slow until my ass has been fully stretched. Also," Lucas stared into Caden's eyes so that he knew that he was being serious, "if at any time you feel overwhelmed or want to stop, you just say so. No questions asked, no feelings hurt. I know this is your first time fucking a man, so if it doesn't end up being your thing, we can stop immediately."

Caden's eyes seemed to soften. He grabbed Lucas's chin between his thumb and index finger. "Thank you," he said before leaning in for a kiss.

Lips locked together, Lucas began to sink down onto Caden's thick cock.

The stretch was real.

Even though they had spent time stretching out his hole, the length and girth of Caden's mega dick had his hole screaming for mercy.

"Holy fuckin' hell," Lucas huffed out as he tried to control his breathing and relax his body. He wasn't a virgin when it came to taking dick, but damn if he didn't feel like one that very moment.

A pair of rough hands grabbed hold of Lucas's hips and held them firm as he continued his attempt at taking the biker's massive dick.

"There." Lucas huffed once his ass was finally seated on Caden's lap.

"Damn, your ass feels so tight."

Yeah, he wondered why that was. Slowly, Lucas began rocking his hips back and forth.

His ass felt so full, it was incredible.

When riding dick, it was all about the angle and switching up of speeds. Long, deep strokes mixed in with short, fast ones. Keeping your top guessing and on edge was what made a bottom so powerful.

Grabbing hold of Caden's muscular shoulders, Lucas began his assault on Caden's dick. He began with long and deep thrusts, gasping each time the man's massive python pressed up against his prostate.

"Fuck, that ass feels so good." Caden moaned, grabbing handfuls of Lucas's ass cheeks and giving them a hard squeeze as he appeared to fall apart.

Staring into Lucas's eyes, Caden began thrusting his cock up into his tight hole. It was hard not to laugh. The man just couldn't help himself. He loved being in control.

Picking up the pace, Lucas rode Caden's dick like his life depended on it.

Moaning and gasping and grunting and clawing. Lucas had never loved riding a dick as much as he loved riding Caden's. The length and the thickness were the perfect combo of stretch and pain.

"Oh god. Right there," Lucas cried out, digging his nails into Caden's back as he held on for dear life.

Stars flashed across his eyes.

The smell of sweat and lust wafted around them.

How was it possible for one man's dick to hit his G-spot so many fucking times. At this rate...

"Jesus, your ass feels too fucking good. I'm not gonna... last... much..." Caden huffed as he continued to fuck upward into Lucas's tight hole.

Crashing their lips together, Lucas lost himself. The need, the intensity, the raw animalistic power. It was all too much for him.

He felt Caden's cock begin to throb inside him.

The man was close.

"Fuck!" Caden shouted, throwing his head back and snapping his hips forward in a violent spasm of pleasure and power.

Feeling Caden come inside him, threw Lucas over the edge. He continued to ride Caden's cock hard and fast, letting out his own scream of ecstasy as he shot his load all over Caden's chiseled stomach.

Their mouths crashed together, breathing in each other's orgasms in a hungry display of passion and lust. Lucas had never felt anything like it. Their bodies couldn't get close enough, their lips never done exploring.

Lucas wasn't sure how long they continued to kiss. All time and space seemed to disappear around them.

Once Caden's cock stopped throbbing inside him, Lucas grabbed the base of his shaft and held the condom in place as he lifted his body off Caden's.

"Jesus, look at that load," Lucas said, holding up the used condom.

Caden chuckled.

"What can I say? You have a magic ass."

Smiling, Lucas wrapped the condom in toilet paper and tossed it into the waste bin next to the sink.

"Now, I think it's time for that bath." Lucas chuckled, leaning over and turning the water back on.

His ass was never going to be the same.

The next morning, Lucas tiptoed into the kitchen. Caden was still sleeping, and he wanted to treat the man to breakfast for once. Ever since he had been staying with Cade, the man had been doing all of the cooking.

He had to admit, for a big, scary bouncer dude, the man knew how to cook.

Pulling open the fridge, he took out the carton of eggs and placed it on the counter next to the sink.

From the corner of his eye, something caught his attention. He turned toward the kitchen window, and his heart caught in his chest.

Sitting on the other side of the windowpane was a ceramic figurine of a hummingbird.

Lucas took a step back and bumped into the kitchen table chair.

"Is everything alright?" Caden asked, causing Lucas to nearly jump out of his skin.

Seeing the terrified look on his face, Caden hurried over and grabbed him by the arms.

"What is it? Is everything okay?"

Lucas stared at the little blue-and-green figurine, speechless and frozen in fear.

Caden followed his gaze toward the window.

"What? The hummingbird? Is that what's got you all riled up?" Lucas nodded. "Oh, it probably belongs to one of my neighbors. Sometimes, kids cut across my backyard instead of walking to the end of the street and going around. Can't tell you how much crap I've found back there left behind by stupid, lazy kids over the years."

Lucas couldn't tear his eyes away from the tiny figure. He hoped and prayed that it was just a coincidence, a terrifying mistake left behind by some ignorant teen.

Because if it wasn't. That meant that this town he had come to love was no longer safe.

Lucas swallowed hard as he continued to stare at the tiny figure of torture.

"So what are we having for breakfast?" Caden asked, his voice barely a whisper compared to the beating of Lucas's heart in his ears.

23

LUCAS

*L*ucas's stomach had been in knots all morning. He couldn't shake this unsettling feeling that he was being watched.

Ever since he saw that fucking hummingbird in the window, his nerves had been on edge.

It had to be all in his head. What were the chances that Darryl had randomly stumbled upon his video among all the millions of crazy videos that were out there online?

Even if he had... somehow... managed to stumble across the video, what were the chances that he would be able to identify the bar and then come and find him in New Mexico?

No. The hummingbird had to be a coincidence, the same as the fire.

Random shit happens all the time.

It didn't mean anything.

He hoped his theories were true.

Not wanting to annoy Caden, Lucas decided to go for a walk to clear his head.

He headed down Main Street with no particular destination in mind. The day was warm, with a slight overcast, perfect for roaming around and worrying about getting a sunburn or overheating. *What was he, seventy? Who worries about "overheating" while taking a walk? Okay, clearly, he wasn't in the right state of mind.*

No matter how hard he tried, his thoughts kept coming back to that damn figurine.

It had to just be a coincidence. There was no way Darryl had found him.

Hummingbird.

The word sent shivers down his spine.

My sweet little hummingbird...

Taking full control, his mind pulled him back through his memories—back to the days when those four little words had meant something so sweet. Four loving words that used to make his heart swoon. Four little words that now brought nothing but fear to his heart.

It was their first weekend getaway together as an official couple. Darryl had surprised Lucas with a weekend stay at this cute little bed-and-breakfast out in Napa Valley.

The place they stayed at was a cozy four-bedroom home that overlooked a small local vineyard. Each morning, a subtle hint of oak wafted through the bedroom window. It was a scent that would always remind Lucas of the walks they took in the overgrown vineyards of Napa Valley.

Lucas had been excited since he found out about their trip.

It was the first time that he would be having a romantic weekend away with his significant other... his boyfriend, if you will.

He loved saying that.

Boyfriend.

He had a boyfriend.

A ruggedly handsome, six-foot-four beast of a man who wanted him. Who enjoyed holding him in his arms, ordering for him at dinner, and even whispering all the nasty, dirty things that he wanted to do to him when they got back to their apartment. The man was a beast when it came to the bedroom. He liked it rough and very controlling. Darryl was the type of man who liked to give orders in bed and expected Lucas to follow instructions to the letter.

Lucas had to admit having such a possessive boyfriend was kind of hot. He knew what he wanted and went after it. Lucas never felt so desired. So wanted.

"What are you staring at, my little hummingbird?"

A smile spread across Lucas's face at the new term of endearment.

"Hummingbird? That's a new one," Lucas replied, without turning from the window.

"It's because my sexy boy never stops singing."

The man could be so sweet.

Darryl stepped up behind him and lowered a tiny figurine in front of Lucas's face.

The porcelain figure twinkled as it spun on the string held between his boyfriend's fingers. Like a master holding a treat *out in front of his dog, Darryl playfully twirled the figurine, trying to entice him.*

"It's beautiful." Lucas gasped, taking the little bird in his hands and holding it out in front of him.

It was a blue-and-black painted ornament of a humming-bird. Its wings were spread wide as it sucked nectar from a sunflower.

"A tiny hummingbird, for my sweet little hummingbird," Darryl repeated, placing a kiss on Lucas's neck.

The man could be so romantic when he wanted to be.

Lucas turned around to face his knight in shining armor.

"I don't know what I did to deserve you," Lucas said, leaning in and giving his man a passionate kiss.

They had been dating for almost two months at that point, long enough for Lucas to fall in love but not long enough for Lucas to discover Darryl's darkness within.

Looking back on everything they had gone through, Lucas still couldn't believe that he had not seen the signs earlier. People really do wear rose-colored glasses when they are in love.

He hated himself for being so blind.

Stopping at the corner, Lucas looked around before proceeding to cross the road. Just as he was about to step onto the pavement, his body froze, and the blood drained from his face.

Standing across the street and next to a row of bushes was a large man wearing solid blue jeans and aviator sunglasses.

Darryl?

Lucas's heart stopped in his chest as panic washed over him.

He was here! He'd found him! He was going to be so mad. Probably take him out to the desert and shoot him.

Men like Darryl didn't like to be disobeyed. Men like Darryl didn't like their things walking out on them.

His heart was racing so fast. He needed to move. To run. Hop on a bus and take off again in another direction.

He was beginning to feel lightheaded.

His vision was starting to blur.

Was he having trouble breathing?

He couldn't remember what he was doing.

"Is everything alright, sir?" a woman's voice asked beside him.

Lucas's vision came back into focus, and he was able to see the woman standing right next to him.

"Huh?" Lucas asked, feeling confused and disoriented.

"Are you alright? You've been staring at that bush for the last five minutes."

Bush? Darryl!

Lucas's head snapped in the direction of the spot where he had last seen his nightmare.

What the?

The street was empty.

Lucas's eyes darted around, desperately trying to locate the man who had made the last few years of his life a living nightmare.

Nothing. No one.

The street was empty.

Had he just imagined seeing his ex standing there? Was it all in his head? Was he actually starting to lose his mind?

Fear will fuck with your mind, that annoying inner voice of his explained.

Get a grip and pull yourself together. Do you think that Cade wants a delusional man hanging around his six-year-old daughter?

Do you think that Caden wants to fuck a man whose head needs to be examined?

Fuck. He was losing it.

"I'm fine. Thank you," Lucas said, quickly stepping across the street and making his way back to Caden's.

So much for clearing your head, Lucas thought to himself.

24

CADEN

The next night, both Caden and Lucas returned to work. Caden worked security while Lucas cleaned tables and helped Alexis switch out kegs.

Everything seemed to be back to normal. Rock music played in the bar as patrons downed beers and shots of alcohol.

Caden decided to conduct a perimeter sweep of the bar. Occasionally, he would find visitors or drunk-as-fuck locals doing things they shouldn't be doing out where anyone could see.

For the bar's sake and reputation, Marcus insisted that any questionable behavior must be conducted out of sight and preferably behind closed doors.

They didn't judge. They just didn't want to get their liquor license revoked or have the bar's name splashed all over social media in a negative light. Ride 'em Hard made too much money to get the place shut down.

Walking around the back of the bar, Caden could hear moaning and grunting.

Shaking his head, he came up behind a man with his pants down around his thighs, ramming some dude hard from behind.

"Sorry, dude. You got to take this to a darker corner or something," Caden said, placing his hand on the guy's shoulder, causing him to pull out of the dude and nearly slap his dick against Caden's thigh as he turned.

The other man remained bent over, hands on the wall in front of him, bare ass spread wide open.

"What the fuck?" Ace shouted, looking over his shoulder, pissed that he was no longer getting rammed into oblivion. "I was almost there, Cade!"

Caught off guard, Caden took a step back.

"Oh shit. Sorry, Ace." Then he realized what he was saying. "Your brother is going to kill you if he catches you fucking out in the open like this. At least go back around the bushes or something," Caden scolded, not caring that he was basically talking to Ace's gaping hole as he glared at him from over his shoulder.

"Argh! Fine!" Ace huffed, yanking his pants up around his waist. "Come. We'll finish off in the back of your truck."

Ace took the confused, burly man by the hand and led him to the far side of the parking lot.

Cade watched as the shirtless muscle daddy opened his truck door and helped Ace inside.

Just before the truck door closed, Ace's hand shot out above the door, giving Caden the finger.

Fuck you, too, you little prick. Caden chuckled to himself as he watched the truck door slam shut and the frame begin rocking.

He walked into the bar through the back entrance and nodded to Marcus as he passed by his boss's office. If he only knew that his little bro was out back getting railed by some muscle daddy, he probably wouldn't be so calm.

Cade grabbed a handful of peanuts and threw them into his mouth as he walked into the main area of the bar.

Lucas was busy wiping down a table and placing an empty beer bottle into the gray bin that he carried with him.

"Busy night?" Caden asked, sliding up next to Lucas.

"Not too crazy. Just cleaning up after these pigs." Lucas huffed, straightening up and stretching out his back. "You seen Ace? He was supposed to help me move some boxes in the back."

Caden looked over his shoulder at the door leading into the back of the bar.

"Umm, he's busy bonding with a customer."

Lucas raised his left eyebrow. "In other words, he's busy getting his prostate examined."

"Yup," Caden responded with a slight chuckle in his voice.

"Hey, Cade?" a rough voice said from behind him.

Cade turned around to see Sheriff Burke standing before him.

"Yeah?" Cade asked, not used to seeing the sheriff in the bar.

If they ever had trouble with customers, Cade and Nikolai always took care of the issue themselves. They never needed to involve the authorities, especially not in gang business.

"I need you to come down to the station to answer a few questions about the fire at Old Man Benson's."

Caden glanced over at Lucas, who looked just as confused as he was.

"Umm, sure, boss. Is everything okay?" Caden asked.

"Yeah, son. Just got a few things to ask you, is all."

"Need me to come as well?" Lucas asked, gripping the cloth in his hand so tight that his knuckles were starting to turn white.

"No, that won't be necessary at this time. Just need to have a quick chat with Cade. Hey, Alexis? You want to tell Marcus that Cade is coming with me and won't be back for the remainder of his shift?"

"Why, boss? That sounds ominous," Caden remarked, not liking how this was beginning to feel.

At that same moment, Marcus emerged from the back, looking annoyed as fuck.

"Is there a problem, Burke?" Marcus asked, crossing his arms against his chest.

"Just taking Cade in for a few follow-up questions. He'll be back in the morning."

Sheriff Burke took Cade by the arm and escorted him from the premises.

How bad could it be if he didn't need handcuffs?

The interrogation room at the jail was nothing more than a tiny room that doubled as a supply closet when not being used. The walls were a dark white, most likely from years of never being cleaned, with shelves that held copy paper, paper towels, and spare mugs used for coffee.

In the center of the room was a rectangular table with two chairs on one side and one chair on the other. There was no hook to restrain criminals to the floor since this jailhouse never really got criminals bad enough to warrant chaining them down.

"Have a seat, Mr. Flanagan. Do you want a coffee?"

"Wow, so formal. Since when don't you call me by my first name?" Caden asked, pulling out the chair and taking a seat.

"This here is official police business, so I'd like to keep it as professional as I can. Mind if we record this?"

"Not without his lawyer present," Marcus said, following them into the interrogation room.

Sheriff Burke looked surprised to see him.

"And when is he or she coming?"

"I called her. She's on her way now." Marcus looked down at his watch. "Probably be here in ten minutes."

"Okay. In that case, I'll make myself a coffee. Want one?"

Both Cade and Marcus shook their heads. They didn't know what was going on, and they wanted to make sure they weren't distracted. Plus, the coffee in the precinct tasted like feet. Both Marcus and Caden had been arrested enough times to know better than to drink the coffee when offered.

Ten minutes later, Cade's lawyer, Ms. Evelyn, arrived, taking the seat next to Caden. The sheriff began his questioning.

"Just want to make this clear: you are not being accused of anything. We just have a few questions we are hoping can clear some things up."

"Sure thing, boss," Caden replied, crossing his hands on the table and sitting up straight. He glanced over at Marcus, who was standing behind the sheriff and leaning against the door.

"What were you doing around four in the morning the day of the fire?"

"Sleeping. Then trying to escape the fire."

"You were sleeping at the barn?" Sheriff Burke asked.

"Yes."

"And why were you sleeping over?"

"We were tired."

"Tired from what?"

Caden looked over at Marcus and his lawyer, who gave him a nod.

"Doing... *adult* things."

The sheriff looked at him for a moment, confused. Then, realization seemed to set in.

"Gotcha. Okay, so what time did you say you woke up in the morning?"

"I don't know. Maybe around four a.m.?" Caden

couldn't remember the exact time, only that it was early and still dark out.

"And why did you wake up?"

"It was getting really hot in the bedroom. When I woke up, the blanket on the bed was on fire, and I could hear Lucas screaming from downstairs."

"And then what happened?"

"I threw the blanket onto the floor, but the damn thing fell on some books Lucas had piled on the floor, and those, too, caught on fire."

"Did you put out the fire upstairs?"

"No, I didn't have time to. Lucas was screaming downstairs. The walls around the bathroom were on fire."

"What about the rest of the barn?"

"What do you mean?" Caden asked, confused.

"Were there other areas of the barn that were on fire as well?"

Caden stopped to think about the questions. Come to think of it, the fires had been on the bedspread and then around the bathroom—nowhere else.

"Just those two areas."

"So there were just the two fires going? The bedroom and the bathroom?" Sheriff Burke asked as if reaching some sordid conclusion.

"What aren't you telling us?" Marcus asked, taking a step forward and glaring at the sheriff.

Sheriff Burke turned to face his old friend.

"The fire marshal has deemed the fire arson. The fires were started at two points of contact. The first was started on the bed where Caden was sleeping. The second was later started outside the bathroom where Lucas was taking a piss."

Caden looked over at Marcus.

"You said in your report that Lucas was trapped in the bathroom and couldn't get the door open?"

Caden nodded.

"Well, it's a good thing you were there. Otherwise, he would have burned to death in that bathroom."

"Arson? You think that someone came into the barn while we were sleeping and set those fires deliberately?" Caden asked, his fist tightening into a ball.

"That's what it's looking like." The sheriff turned his focus back on Cade. "Look, I've known you since you were a little tyke. I know that you're incapable of killing someone so sweet."

Caden noticed that the sheriff limited his comment to "someone so sweet," not that he was incapable of killing people in general. Did that mean that the sheriff believed that he was capable of killing people only if they were bad?

He wasn't quite sure whether he should take that as a compliment or an insult.

"Can you think of anyone who would want to do you or Lucas any harm?" the sheriff asked, flipping through his notepad and reading through his notes.

Caden glanced at Marcus. There was no way in hell that he was telling Burke who he suspected might have been behind the fire. But if his suspicions were right, he wanted the Shadow Vipers to deliver their justice.

Someone had tried to kill them. Someone was about to die.

"None that I can think of," Caden finally said, giving Marcus the "we need to talk" look.

"Do you have any further questions, Sheriff?" Marcus asked, standing up straight and getting ready to leave.

The sheriff studied Caden's face for a few moments before lowering his gaze and shaking his head. "No. I think we're done for now."

"Thank you, Sheriff," Caden said, standing up and shaking Burke's hand.

After exiting the building, they watched as Ms. Evelyn hopped into her BMW, waving as she drove off.

"Okay, spill it," Marcus snarled once they were alone on the street.

The man looked terrifying when he was pissed as shit.

"Well, I have no proof or anything, and perhaps I might be wrong, but I think it might have been Lucas's ex who set fire to the barn."

"His ex?" Marcus asked.

"Yes. The guy was emotionally and physically abusive, and Lucas had to escape by drugging the guy and running off in the night. I don't know much about the asshole, just that he is dangerous and connected."

"Connected, how? As in mob-connected or politics-connected?"

"Connected as in he is a cop with a lot of corrupt friends."

Marcus looked lost in thought as he gazed into the

distance. Caden had noticed him like this before, especially when he was plotting a job or considering a complex next move.

"Okay, for now, we keep this shit to ourselves. I'll see what I can dig up about Lucas and his ex."

Caden agreed. There was no point in telling Lucas and having him worry if it turned out to be nothing in the end.

The fire was suspicious.

25

LUCAS

*T*hings were starting to get out of control. Everywhere Lucas turned, he swore he saw his ex —at the grocery store, at the park, even waiting in line to get coffee, three customers up. It was getting to the point where Lucas was ready to check himself into a mental institution. How much paranoia could one mind take?

Then there was Caden. Ever since Sheriff Burke hauled him in to ask him a few questions, he'd been acting all secretive and shifty.

It was the kind of shifty that married men became right before they got busted for cheating on their wives—or husbands.

Caden was hiding something, and Lucas wanted to know what the fuck it was.

Sitting in a booth, he picked at the blueberry muffin he'd been working on for the past hour. His body might be sitting in Mona's Café, but his mind was a million miles away.

What if Darryl really had found him? Where would he run off to next?

Thanks to the fire, he didn't have any money saved, and he wasn't really sure where he could run that Darryl wouldn't be able to find him.

Things were beginning to feel hopeless.

Lucas's head snapped up when he heard someone call out his name.

"Lucas?" the woman behind the counter asked. "Is your name Lucas?"

She was wearing an apron that announced her name was Jill, possibly the owner of this establishment, but Lucas really wasn't sure.

"Yes, that's me," Lucas answered, confused.

The woman held out a phone to him and shrugged her shoulders. "You have a phone call."

"Me?" Lucas asked, still confused by the situation.

Caden had bought him a replacement cell phone, so if it were him on the phone, he would have called him on that.

"Yes. They asked to speak to Lucas, the guy wearing the teal shirt and eating a muffin."

His heart stopped in his chest, and all the air was suddenly sucked from his lungs.

He couldn't breathe.

The world around him had suddenly fallen silent.

The woman's lips continued to move, but the only sound Lucas could hear was the deafening pounding of his heart in his ears.

He found me.

That was the only thought he was able to generate.

The woman held the phone closer, waiting for him to take it.

He was calling on the phone.

That had to be a good thing. If Darryl had wanted him dead, he would have shot him in the head while he played with his muffin.

That *had* to mean that Darryl didn't want to make a scene.

Holding his breath, Lucas stood from his seat and slowly walked over to the counter.

The woman gave him a dirty look, most likely annoyed that he was wasting her time. She shoved the phone into his hand, then walked back over to serve the next customer.

Lucas brought the phone to his ear with a trembling hand and listened.

"Hello, my sweet little *hummingbird*," the voice hissed through the line. "It's been a long time. How have you been?" Darryl's deep voice came through the receiver, sending chills down Lucas's spine.

Closing his eyes, he was too terrified to look up and around the coffee shop. His ex had to be close. He knew where he was and what he was wearing.

"Glad to see that I can still take your breath away," his ex added with a snarl.

"Wh-what do you want?" Lucas finally managed. His heart was pounding, and his knees were shaking.

The last time he'd seen Darryl, Lucas had drugged him, then run off while he was passed out. Men like Darryl didn't do well with being tricked or disobeyed. Men like Darryl got revenge.

What was his ex going to do to him if he ever got ahold of him? That was a question he hoped to never have answered.

All around him, people went about their business—ordering coffees and chatting with their friends. The rest of the world was oblivious to the nightmare unfolding right next to the counter.

"I've come to collect you. The last time we were together, you left without saying *goodbye*." There was something dark and sinister in the way Darryl pronounced the word "good-bye"—as if it carried a finality instead of the possibility of seeing one another again in the future.

Lucas felt like he was going to be sick.

Gathering his courage, he opened his eyes and slowly glanced around the café, scanning the faces and bodies of all those sitting around him, trying to locate a monster hiding in sheep's clothing.

"It... it's over, Darryl. I'm not coming back." He tried to sound firm and hoped his voice would come across as confident. But he knew that Darryl would see through his pathetic attempt. He knew that Lucas was not strong—he was weak and scared and unable to stand up for himself, especially when faced with an alpha male.

Lucas listened to the voice on the other end *tsk-tsk* before breathing in a breath of air.

"My sweet, little *hummingbird*. What makes you think I would ever let you go? You're mine, and I've come to collect what belongs to *me*."

He couldn't go back. He couldn't go back to living a life of constant fear and humiliation—a life in which he degraded himself to the orders and commands of a person who didn't respect him.

"Never. Leave me alone," Lucas growled, hating the fear building up inside him. His ex still had so much power over him.

"It's funny that you think you have a choice in the matter."

Lucas scanned the front of the café, wondering if perhaps his ex was waiting for him outside.

"We can do this the easy way or the terrifyingly hard way," his ex snarled over the line.

Lucas's skin went cold.

"*Yes*... now I've got your attention. If we do this the easy way, you say your goodbyes this afternoon and pack some things before heading out with me tonight. The other... more gruesome way... involves me removing your boyfriend's eyes with my hunting knife before I take his little daughter swimming out in a lake late at night. Tell me, *sweet* hummingbird. Which way would you prefer?"

Panic spread over Lucas like he had never experienced before.

It was one thing to hurt him. He was used to it and could endure the torture if need be. But it was another to hurt Cade and Lizzy. They were both innocent in all of this, and there was no way in hell he would allow Darryl to harm either of them.

They needed to be protected.

"Time is ticking," he said before pausing for what felt like an eternity. "I'll be in touch."

The line went dead.

Slowly, Lucas returned the phone to the base on the wall of the café. The time had come for him to make a decision. Run once again or face his fears.

26

CADEN

amn, it." Caden huffed, ending his call and stuffing his phone into his jeans pocket.

Something was wrong.

He had been trying to reach Lucas all day, but his phone kept going straight to voicemail.

Lucas had decided to go to the coffee shop this morning to grab a drink and clear his head. Caden had offered to go with him, but Lucas had insisted that he needed some alone time and would be back in a couple of hours.

That was eight hours ago.

There had been no call, no text, no stopping by the house to say that he was okay. Just radio silence.

Caden was worried... and a little pissed.

He walked into Ride 'em Hard, hoping to find Lucas sitting at the bar, enjoying a drink with Ace.

No such luck.

"Hey, Alexis. Have you seen Lucas?" Caden asked, the

pit of worry in his stomach growing with every minute that passed.

Alexis swirled around, her blonde-and-pink hair slapping against her cheek as she turned. In her hand, she held a pint glass that she was busy drying with a hand towel.

She gave Caden a once-over before deciding that his appearance really didn't matter to her. He was off-duty, so he had just thrown on a pair of ripped jeans and a muscle shirt before leaving the house. He was worried about Lucas and in a hurry to get to the bar.

"Yeah, he was here about two hours ago. Grabbed something from the back, then left. I think he was heading home to see you."

He hadn't.

Wherever he had gone, it wasn't to Caden's house.

He checked his phone once again.

Nothing.

"Look, can you ask Nikolai to cover for me tonight? I'm gonna run home and see if he is there. He's not answering his phone, and I'm starting to get worried about him."

Alexis gave him a sympathetic look.

"Did you guys have a fight?"

Caden shook his head.

"Well, if it makes you feel better, he didn't say anything nasty about you." She chuckled.

That didn't make Caden feel any better.

He thanked Alexis and then left the bar in a hurry.

When he arrived home, the kitchen light was on. Hopefully, that meant that Lucas was home.

"Luc?" Caden called as he pushed open the door.

"In here," Lucas answered from somewhere inside the kitchen.

Relief flooded Caden's insides. The man was safe. Thank god.

"Where have you been? I've been calling you all day." Caden asked, walking into the kitchen and giving Lucas a kiss on the cheek.

Lucas was standing by the stove, plating up some steaks.

"Sorry, my cell phone died, and I had to run some errands. Didn't mean to worry you."

"It's alright. Was just worried, is all."

Lucas passed Cade an open bottle of beer, then took a sip of his own red wine.

"Thanks, babe. Dinner smells great."

"Perfect timing. Dinner's ready," Lucas noted, carrying their plates to the kitchen table.

Caden carried his beer and Lucas's wine to the table and sat down in his usual spot. Lucas sat down across from him.

Something was off about Lucas. He was quieter than usual and had trouble making eye contact with Cade.

"Cheers," Lucas whispered, raising his glass and then taking several gulps of his wine. Caden followed suit. It was rude to stop drinking while the other person was still going.

He had heard that was a thing. Perhaps an Irish folktale or European superstition. Someone had told him once that one was supposed to keep eye contact with their drinking buddy and only stop drinking once the other person did so as well.

Or something like that.

He never questioned it before because, hey, who didn't love drinking?

"So, how was your day?" Lucas finally asked, glancing up briefly before diverting his eyes once again.

Something was up.

There was a struggle in his eyes, something he was trying to keep hidden from the world. If Caden had just met Lucas, he might not have noticed. But now, Caden was an expert when it came to reading Lucas's tells.

The boy was hiding something, and he was feeling awfully guilty about whatever it was.

"My day was spent trying to locate you," Caden said, annoyed and a tiny bit suspicious. Caden cut into his steak and shoved a piece into his mouth.

Flavors and juices exploded all over his tongue. He had no idea that Lucas was such a fantastic cook. *God, if the boy could make such a delicious-tasting steak, what else was he amazing at cooking?*

Taking another bite of his steak, he watched as Lucas still refused to look him in the eye.

"Yeah, I'm really sorry about that." Lucas took another sip of his wine, looking uncomfortably to his left as he drank.

He finally turned and locked eyes with Caden. He swallowed hard, appearing nervous as fuck.

"That's one of the things that I love about you, Cade. You're always looking out for me." He smiled, then raised his glass. "Cheers."

Lucas waited for Cade to raise his beer as well.

They both drank together.

Taking another breath, the boy continued.

"Before I met you, I didn't think that I could ever feel this way again. You gave me hope. You showed me what it was like to be equals. To have my opinions valued and to feel safe and cared about." Lucas looked down at his glass of wine. "For that, I will always be grateful."

Why was Lucas talking in the past tense?

"I know that Darryl is in town." Lucas's voice was suddenly cold. Gone was the nervous, stammering boy Caden had spoken to only a few moments ago.

"What? Where?" Caden growled, jumping to his feet.

A wave of vertigo hit Caden, and he grabbed the table quickly for support. The walls around him began to sway, and his body was beginning to feel all floaty.

"Sit back down, Cade. I don't want you getting hurt."

He was back to not making eye contact. Lucas took another sip of his wine and waited.

Caden slumped back into his seat, clutching the table for support.

"He gave me an ultimatum. Either I leave with him tonight quietly, or he will kill you and Lizzy."

Caden's eyes went wide when he realized what was happening.

Lucas stood, downing the last little bit of his wine.

"I love you too much to see any harm come to either one of you."

Caden's vision was starting to get blurry. He struggled to focus on the man standing across from him.

"I'm leaving with Darryl," Lucas announced, taking a step backward. "I'm going to end this thing one way or another."

"Lucas! No!" Caden tried to argue. He lifted his arm, which felt like a million pounds.

He glanced at Lucas's food, which remained untouched, and then at his own. *That little fucker...*

"I slipped a little something into your beer. You'll be fine when you wake up. I just need a head start."

Lucas walked around the table and stopped right next to Cade.

"I love you, Cade," he confessed before bending down and kissing his cheek ever so softly.

Lucas was sacrificing himself and his happiness in order to protect Caden and his daughter. Caden's heart cried out in pain.

"Lucas..." Caden whispered as his body slumped forward on the table.

Lucas ran his hand through Caden's hair one final time before turning and walking toward the kitchen door.

With his body slumped across the table, Caden watched the blurry image of Lucas fade into the darkness.

His eyes became heavy, and he could no longer fight the pull.

Blackness enveloped him as he sank into the world beneath him.

"*A*rgh," Caden groaned as he slowly lifted his head off the kitchen table. His arm was soaked from his spilled beer, and his neck was feeling tight as fuck—most likely from passing out at a weird angle.

Rubbing the back of his neck, he looked around the kitchen. The lights were still on, and it was still dark outside.

Raising his left arm, he glanced at the watch he wore—yes, he was one of those guys who used a watch to tell time.

Ten thirty p.m.

Good, he hadn't been out for that long. He was guessing that he'd only passed out for about two and a half hours.

Staring at the untouched dinner sitting across from him, he cursed. "Fuck!"

Caden got to his feet, still feeling groggy and disoriented. He grabbed his keys and rushed out back, hoping against all hope that he would find Lucas still standing in his backyard.

The place was empty.

He stumbled around the house and jumped onto his motorcycle. He wasn't in the best condition to drive, but this was an emergency, and Lucas's life was in danger. He needed to get to the guys.

Shoving the keys into the bike, he pressed the start button and listened to the beast roar to life. The cycle was louder than usual as if sensing that it needed to perform at its optimum that night. Its master's love was in danger, and the beast had one job to do—get her owner to his destination in record time.

Connecting his phone to Bluetooth, Cade said Marcus's name out loud, activating the voice call on his cell.

A minute later, a growly man answered.

"Boss, we got a problem," Caden snarled as he kicked the bike in gear and sped off down the street.

Fifteen minutes later, he came to a screeching halt in front of the bar and snarled at Nikolai as he marched on by.

Ace met him at the door and signaled for Blade, who followed Cade and Nikolai into the back of the bar.

Marcus was waiting for them, huddled over a stainless steel table, scrolling through his tablet while chatting with his phone on speaker.

"Yeah, he just arrived. I'll call you back in a few." Marcus stabbed his phone with his finger and then locked eyes with Cade. "We're going to get him back."

"And I'm going to bury that motherfucker," Caden snarled. He had never been so pissed before in his life.

"Sheriff Burke is checking out security camera feeds to

see if he can locate Luc and that asshole ex of his. I'll call him back after we decide on a plan."

"Hunt asshole, murder asshole. Sounds like a plan to me," Caden growled, punching his fist into the table.

Ace grabbed Cade by the shoulder, trying to offer him some comfort. "That asshole messed with the wrong crew. We're going to get our boy back and dismember the fucker."

Caden nodded to Ace over his shoulder. He appreciated that all the guys had his back, and he loved all the murder suggestions being made. This was brotherhood. This was family. They stuck together and helped one another. No judgment and no questions asked.

Alexis came rushing into the back room. "Is it true? Was Lucas kidnapped?"

She looked worried and scared and couldn't stop shaking her head in disbelief.

"Yes. But we're going to get him back," Marcus cut in.

"Do you think it had anything to do with why Lucas was here earlier?" Alexis asked.

They all looked at Alexis, confused.

Cade had totally forgotten that Lucas had stopped by the bar for some unknown reason earlier in the day.

What had he been doing? And if he was going to leave town, why stop by his place of work?

It just didn't make any sense.

Neither did drugging him and leaving town with his psycho ex-boyfriend.

"Boss, can we check the cameras to see what Luc was up

to earlier today?" Caden asked, the pit in his stomach tightening.

With each minute they wasted, Luc and his ex got further away. They needed to find him.

"Yeah, that's a smart move," Marcus noted, straightening up and motioning for Cade and Ace to follow him.

They all crowded into Marcus's office and huddled around his laptop as he scrolled through the bar's surveillance feeds.

It didn't take them long to find Lucas. He entered the bar just after three, then headed downstairs into the basement. Then they watched as Lucas walked over to the lamp that hung on the wall and turned it, causing the hidden wall to shift, giving him access to the area Marcus had restricted for crew business only.

"I thought only a select few knew about the room?" Marcus grumbled, glancing over at Cade and giving him a stern look.

Marcus could punish him later, but right now, he needed to focus on the boy's movements.

Once in the hidden room, they watched as Lucas picked up a cloth sack and...

Caden's eyes went wide as he watched the once sweet and innocent man collect his instruments of death. He wasn't sure what the boy's intentions were, but judging by what he was collecting, it probably wasn't good.

Closing the wall behind him, Lucas crept back up the stairs and exited the bar using the back exit. He didn't say goodbye or even glance over his shoulder. He was solely focused on the steps in front of him.

"It appears that our boy has a plan of his own," Marcus noted, pressing pause on the video feed.

"What do you think he is going to do?" Ace asked, looking a little green in the face.

"Nothing good, I'm afraid." Marcus turned to Cade. "Who knew your boy was so dark? Make sure you don't ever forget an anniversary or birthday, bud."

Caden gave him a glare. This wasn't the time for jokes.

"We need to rescue him," Caden said, slamming the laptop closed and straightening up.

"I hate to tell you, Cade, but I think we all underestimated that bashful little twink. Something tells me he is a lot more dangerous than we give him credit for."

At that moment, Marcus's phone rang.

"It's the sheriff."

28

LUCAS

*A*s predicted, once Lucas finished drugging Caden and stepped outside the house, Darryl was waiting. He'd been sitting in a shitty unremarkable car that most people wouldn't even notice, watching the house like any high-functioning stalker.

Lucas was used to his ex's obsessive behavior. In the beginning, he thought it was cute, his boyfriend waiting for him or surprising him when he was out getting a coffee with friends. But as time went on, the possessiveness became something out of a horror movie.

He was not allowed to hang out with his friends. On the rare occasions that he was able to convince Darryl to let him go meet up with some people, his ex would magically show up or wait for him in the parking lot or some other creepy location.

Darryl even monitored his timing and movements. God forbid Lucas deviated from his schedule or stopped off at a store to pick something up unexpectedly. He would get berated when he got home and accused of cheating on his ex. Those nights always ended with hours of pleading and trying to convince his ex that he was not unfaithful and that he still loved him.

It wasn't until the end that Lucas realized how toxic their relationship really had been. By then, leaving his ex was nearly impossible.

Things really got scary when Darryl convinced his cop buddies to slowly patrol the area.

The police culture, especially in LA, was a big old boys' club. They looked out for one another and did what was necessary to protect each other. That was one of the reasons Lucas had been so careful not to use any sort of technology or service that might create a digital trail or allow Darryl to somehow find him. He hadn't been counting on somebody videotaping him and then posting it online without his permission.

People really needed to think before they posted. Life was more than just *likes* and *followers*.

Sadly, that mindless drone mentality was sweeping across the nation.

People didn't question things or verify accusations for themselves. They just simply believed whatever popular rumor was being spread and jumped on the social media bandwagon, participating in the latest trend or vilifying or canceling people without using their brains to discover the truth for themselves. Nobody thought about the consequences of their posts.

If only he had seen the warning signs. But when you are being emotionally and psychologically abused, you don't even realize it is happening. You somehow convince yourself that it is your fault and that you are overreacting. It isn't until your first black eye or accidental broken jaw that you realize perhaps Prince Charming isn't really so charming.

And now, here he was. Voluntarily getting into a car with his ex. A man he had spent months running from. Willingly sticking his head in the lion's mouth and praying that the beast didn't bite down.

But this time, it was different.

Knowing that Caden and Lizzy's lives were in danger, an inner monster awoke inside of him. He was no longer driven by fear. He was now driven by the need to protect those he loved. Yes, he loved his beefy biker dude and his kindhearted little munchkin. He hoped that perhaps they could have a future one day. If only he were able to survive this ordeal.

Well, he wasn't going to get ahead of himself.

One way or another, this nightmare was going to end.

They had been driving for about two hours west, most likely on their way back to Los Angeles. Darryl had come to collect him, after all. If he had wanted to kill him, Darryl would have done it long ago.

No. With Darryl, it was all about control and possession. He needed to remind Lucas who was in charge. He needed to make sure that Lucas felt fear and understood that there was no escaping him. Abusive men were narcissistic assholes who needed to maintain their power in order to feel good about themselves.

"It's getting late. We should probably stop at a hotel for the night," Lucas suggested. It was a fifteen-hour drive from New Mexico to LA, and he doubted Darryl was planning on driving all the way back in one night.

Darryl snorted. "Like hell I'm checking us into a hotel for the night. Think I'm stupid? The minute we check in, you'll be planning your escape."

Lucas rolled his eyes. "So your plan is to drive straight through until we get home?"

Pitch-black eyes landed on Lucas. Once, he had found those eyes so mesmerizing and charming. Now, they were just a reminder of the monster that waited to devour him.

"Since when did you get such a smart mouth?"

There was an underlying tone to his voice that warned Lucas to choose his words carefully. Darryl didn't have an issue cracking him one against the jaw if it put him back in line.

Lucas watched as Darryl's grip tightened on the steering wheel.

"We're spending the night camping in the desert," Darryl snarled. He appeared irritated that Lucas had questioned his actions. It might have been a few months since they'd seen each other, but Darryl was expecting him to fall back in line immediately.

Eventually, they left the interstate and followed a long dirt road that appeared to lead to nowhere.

Fifteen minutes later, they came to a large clearing, perfect for camping.

"Get your ass out of the car and help," Darryl ordered,

throwing the car in park before adjusting the ballcap on his head that hid his handsome features.

How could a man who had such gorgeous features be nothing but rotten on the inside?

Huffing, Lucas exited and began unloading the car as ordered. In the trunk, he found a cooler and two sleeping bags. It appeared that Darryl had planned this little excursion beforehand.

Made sense. Cops were always thinking ahead. That's how they survived gang takedowns and homicidal men with machetes.

While Darryl was temporarily distracted trying to collect usable wood to start a fire, Lucas pulled out the knapsack he had bought from the house and carefully placed it next to the other items he had unpacked from the car.

He then walked over to where his ex was crouched down, attempting to light a fire.

It had been forever since they last camped together, and Darryl still sucked at lighting campfires. But there was no way he was going to remind Darryl of that fact.

"Need me to grab anything?" Lucas offered, trying to remain on Darryl's good side.

"Yeah, there are some sandwiches in the cooler, and you can grab me a beer as well."

Lucas did as he was told, ever the good listener.

Once the fire was roaring, Darryl sat down next to Lucas and offered him a bite from his sandwich. Lucas shook his head.

"So when did you find me?" Lucas asked, staring into the fire as the flames danced over the wood.

"A little over two weeks ago. A coworker of mine saw that video of you singing that was posted online. It took me a bit of time to figure out which bar it was, but I happened to glimpse a reflection of the bar's name in one of the windows in the background. It was just a quick snapshot, so I almost missed it. After that, it was only a matter of time before I was able to confirm that you were, in fact, in New Mexico. I arrived in town about a week ago."

"You've been in town for a week?" Lucas gasped, snapping his head toward his bastard of an ex.

"Yes. I had to do a little recon first. See what it was that my little hummingbird was up to. Then I saw you with... *him.*"

"Did you start the fire?" Lucas asked, already knowing the answer.

Darryl nodded. "That asshole thought he could take what was mine."

Trying to keep his emotions in check, Lucas clenched his jaw and focused on the flames before him. He needed to remain calm.

A rough, meaty paw slid across his lap and settled on his hand. Darryl gave Lucas's hand a squeeze.

"Don't worry, my little hummingbird. In time, I'll forgive you for what you've done. Betraying my love like that. Leaving me and then sleeping with that miscreant of a man. If you can even call him that. Tomorrow, we'll be back home, and then you can begin earning back my respect and my trust."

Hearing Darryl's words made Lucas's blood boil. This was how psychological manipulation began. Trying to make the victim feel like it was their fault and that somehow they owed it to their abuser to make things right.

Like hell. There was no fucking way he was ever going back to that life.

Tonight, it all ended, one way or another.

"Grab me another beer," his ex ordered, tossing the empty bottle on the dirt beside them.

Lucas stood up, taking a step past the man he had grown to hate.

Slap!

Darryl's hand smacked Lucas's ass with all the power he had remembered.

Without thinking, Lucas spun around and slapped his ex across the face.

Lucas froze. His eyes went wide when he realized what he had just done. He hadn't meant to slap his ex; it was just a natural reaction to someone slapping your ass without your permission.

Rage flashed across Darryl's eyes.

He knew what was coming next.

In an instant, Darryl was on his feet, grabbing Lucas by the throat. His big, meaty fingers dug into Lucas's soft flesh.

Flashes appeared of all the past assaults, all the bruises, broken jaw, and even dislocated shoulder from when he had lost track of time and ended up coming home from rehearsals three hours too late. Darryl had been fuming that night. He chased Lucas into their apartment stairwell before grabbing him hard by the arm and shoving him down the stairs. He didn't go to a hospital that night. Instead, he stayed with a dislocated shoulder for six hours until Darryl brought one of his cop buddies over to reset his shoulder.

Cops looking out for cops. There was a code of silence they all lived by.

Lucas struggled, clawing at Darryl's hands as they tightened around his throat.

"I'm going to teach you respect once again, *boy*. You've been running wild for way too long for my liking," his ex snarled into his ear. "It's time I remind you who's in charge here."

Lights flashed across Lucas's eyes as Darryl's fist connected with his cheek. He held his breath, waiting for the next blow. There was always a second blow.

Right on schedule, Lucas keeled over when his ex's fist landed in his gut.

Fingers digging into the dirt beneath him, he tried to catch his breath.

Anger began to build. He needed to remain calm and in control. If he went at Darryl with all that he had, Darryl would have him pinned on his back and broken in a matter of minutes. His ex was a beast of a man and outweighed Lucas by at least sixty pounds.

No. Lucas needed to play things right, submit, and regain his ex's trust and confidence. He needed his ex to believe he had won and that Lucas was his once again.

Hunched over on all fours, Lucas tried to regain control of his breathing once again.

You can do this. You need to submit. You need to show him that he's in control and that you are his to command once again.

Swallowing down his dignity, he whispered, "I'm sorry. I'll do better next time."

"Damn right, you will. Now, get up and get me that beer I asked for."

Lucas struggled to his feet and made his way over to the cooler. He popped open the lid and fished out a cold one for his ex.

"That's a good boy," Darryl noted, taking the beer from Lucas once he returned. "Come. Sit." He patted the log right beside him before cracking open his beer and taking a long swig.

Staring into the fire, the next few hours seemed to pass unnoticed. It was only after Darryl added some more wood to the diminishing flames that Lucas's mind finally returned to his body.

"Love, I'm starting to get a bit of a headache. Do you mind grabbing the bottle of painkillers out of my knapsack over there?" Lucas asked, knowing that the term of endearment would break through Darryl's defenses. There was nothing like a compliment to stroke a man's inflated ego.

Judging by the smile that spread across Darryl's face, Lucas knew that Darryl's defenses were down. Plus, the alcohol was a nice added touch.

The man walked over to where their supplies were lying and crouched down in front of Lucas's knapsack.

"See, babe. I knew that deep down you still loved me," Darryl said, smiling at Lucas as he pulled open the knapsack without looking.

The man yelped and jumped back as two of the hidden rattlesnakes jumped out at Darryl and bit him.

Shouting, he threw one of the snakes against a rock just as the third snake jumped out and bit him on the neck.

Darryl cried out and shouted, arms flailing as he tried to fend off the attacking snakes. He lost his balance and fell to the ground, trying to scramble away with no success.

Lucas watched as the two snakes attacked his ex, their tails rattling as they continued their ferocious assault against the man who had disturbed their slumber.

A wicked grin spread across Lucas's face as his ex's body writhed around on the ground in pain. His face and arms were beginning to swell, and his screams were becoming stifled and hard to understand.

Had his ex been bitten by one snake, his chances of survival—with the right medical treatment—may have been possible. But this poor soul had been bitten by three snakes multiple times and would not be receiving any medical treatment tonight or anytime soon.

Taking a bite of his sandwich, Lucas watched as the two snakes joined their brother and slithered off into the darkness of the desert around them.

"Lu... Lu... hel...p." Darryl's voice was nothing more

than a wheeze. So different from the powerful beast he had once been.

Swallowing the last of his sandwich, Lucas stood up and walked over to where his monster of an ex lay, swollen, bleeding, and gasping for air.

His face was majorly swollen, and one of his eyes didn't open at all. Large lumps and red marks peppered his arms, a clear map of the deadly assault he had endured.

Standing over his dying ex, Lucas looked down with coldness in his eyes. He never considered himself an evil man, but tonight's actions were a clear confirmation that the devil lives inside all of us. Some have the strength to keep him at bay, while others eventually give up and let the *Prince of Darkness* out to play.

"I'm sorry that it had to come to this. There was no way that I was ever giving you that sort of power over me again. Had it just been me you threatened, I might have let you live. I probably would have framed you for some crime or made sure you had some sort of non-life-threatening accident that punished you but got you out of my life. But when you threatened the lives of Caden and his sweet little girl, that was when I realized a monster like you needs to be put down."

Lucas walked around Darryl's body as he continued to struggle to breathe through his swollen throat.

"At some point tomorrow, a police officer will stumble across me and hear about how you kidnapped me and tried to take me home with you. Thankfully, you accidentally stumbled across a nest of rattlesnakes, startling them and causing them to attack. I, being lost in the middle of nowhere with no cell phone or ability to help, watched helplessly as you struggled and died from their poisonous venom. A horrific, tragic way to die."

Lucas glared down at his ex. He watched as the man struggled to take his last few breaths. Still, he felt nothing. No sorrow. No regret. If anything, he felt a tinge of pleasure that justice had finally been served.

This was a man who had spent so many years causing him fear and pain and doing everything in his power to maintain control over his life and physical being.

Darryl would not be missed. Monsters like him deserved to be slain in the cold darkness of the night—alone and withering in extreme pain.

"Goodbye, Darryl. Thank you for teaching me how to be strong."

Standing in the glow of the fire, Lucas watched as the last glimmer of life faded from his ex's eyes.

His monster was dead.

29

CADEN

*H*anging up the phone, Marcus looked up at Cade.

"He's been spotted on a surveillance camera at a gas station an hour west of here. The sheriff's got contacts in the area trying to get security footage to see if they can track their movements."

A surge of hope jolted through Caden.

They had a lead!

"Well, let's get moving!" Caden shouted, jumping to his feet.

"Cade," Marcus called before Caden had a chance to leave the room. "We need to be prepared for what we might find."

Caden looked over at his boss and friend. He wasn't willing to entertain any outcome other than the one in which Lucas was standing alive and well.

"Luc will be okay. You'll see. He's a lot stronger than he appears."

Marcus shook his head.

"That's not what I meant. If Lucas was successful in whatever plan he had concocted, there is a very real chance that he may have murdered his ex. Depending on who arrives at the scene first, we might be looking at a possible murder charge."

"No. That's not happening. I don't care who finds him; he's not going to jail for defending himself."

Ace stepped forward. "We need to make sure that Sheriff Burke is the one who finds Lucas first. Burke won't let anything happen to him. He's always helped to protect the crew and our community."

"Good point," Marcus said, walking over to where Caden was waiting. "You deal with Burke, and I'll let the boys know we are going hunting."

Fifteen minutes later, Marcus and his crew hopped on their bikes and began their journey west. They had loaded up on weapons: guns, bats, and brass knuckles—which were Nikolai's weapon of choice. The man loved using his hands for pain as well as pleasure.

Blade, of course, grabbed his trove of knives. There wasn't a murder he committed that didn't involve one of his blades, hence the nickname.

Caden grabbed a gun as well as a hunting knife. He wasn't sure what they would be walking into, but if he was able to get up close and personal with Lucas's ex, he wouldn't mind plunging the knife into the man's gut. Perhaps see how deep he could get the blade before pulling the man's intestines out through his stomach. The thought of murdering the man who had hurt his love made him feel all warm and tingly inside.

Throughout the ride, Ace kept in touch with Sheriff Burke, providing updates to Marcus and Caden as they rode to their boy's rescue.

It didn't take long for one of Burke's contacts to spot Darryl's vehicle exiting the interstate on one of their CCTV cameras and heading down toward a deserted area.

Burke thanked his contact and informed him that backup would not be needed as he had the situation well under control.

Exiting the interstate, Marcus led the hoard of bikers toward a flickering red glow off in the distance. It had to be Lucas's campfire.

It wasn't until Cade was faced with the possibility of losing Luc that he realized he couldn't live without him. He no longer cared what others would think. He had found someone who made him smile and feel good and always lit up the room whenever he entered.

A world in which Luc was not a part of was too horrible to imagine.

The thunderous roar of all of their bikes came to a halt once they reached the makeshift campsite. Dirt and dust kicked up into the air, adding to the eerie silence of the open space around them.

Throwing his leg over his bike, Caden ran to where Lucas was sitting, motionless, staring at the fire.

"Luc!" Caden shouted, dropping to his knees in front of the boy. "I'm here. Are you okay?"

Lucas's warm brown eyes slowly drifted toward Cade. It took a few seconds before recognition finally set in.

A smile slowly spread across Lucas's face.

"Cade. You came after me." Lucas lunged forward and wrapped his arms around Cade. He clung to him firmly, like he was afraid Cade would disappear.

"Of course I did," Caden whispered into his ear, holding him tight and never wanting to let go. Then he remembered. "Where's your ex?" Cade asked, quickly pulling away and glancing around the area.

"Dude! His face! It's like popcorn! Like, seriously. What the fuck did that to him?" Ace shouted from somewhere off to their right.

"A snake bite. Three of them. Over and over," Lucas muttered without showing much emotion.

The eerie calmness to his voice had Caden a little worried.

"Are you okay?" Caden asked, hoping for a little more than just a generic response.

Lucas stared up into his eyes and slowly smiled.

"Yes, I'm great." He reached over and took Caden's hand. "Have I ever told you that I love you?"

Caden laughed.

"Yeah, I kind of remember you saying that... right after you drugged me."

Lucas chuckled. "Nothing says 'I love you' quite like slipping something into your boyfriend's drink to protect his sexy ass."

"I think next time, I'd prefer not to be drugged. Messes with my macho-man ego."

They both chuckled. Lucas leaned forward and gently kissed Cade on his lips.

"Like seriously. This dude's face is fucking *disgusting*. Remind me never to piss you off, Lucas. Cade, your boyfriend is a fucking nutjob."

"I wouldn't have him any other way."

"You may have to promote him from busboy to enforcer, boss," Blade added, bending down next to Ace, looking on with fascination.

"Are we seriously going to ignore the fact that Lucas just called Cade his boyfriend?" Marcus joked. "I think I may have to get you both to sign a disclosure or something."

"Yeah, no fucking on the job," Ace chirped, glancing up at Caden while poking Lucas's ex with a stick.

"Hey, I wasn't the one getting railed by that daddy in the back of his truck," Caden defended.

Marcus turned his judging eyes toward his younger brother and crossed his arms against his chest.

"You were getting what?" Marcus asked, in that big-brother tone that he liked to use to piss off his little bro.

Blade stepped back and away from Ace.

"Hey, this isn't about me or my ass. This is about Caden violating Lucas's ass whenever he feels like it," Ace chirped back.

"Hey, who's to say that it's not me violating Caden's ass whenever I want?" Lucas spoke up from under Cade's arm.

The group turned and gave a judging eye to Luc. It was clear that no one believed a word coming from the boy's mouth.

"What? It could happen," Lucas tried to defend.

"Sure it could, love," Ace said, returning to poking the popcorn man lying in front of him. "Just like I could suddenly become an aggressive top and pop Blade's cherry when he's had a few drinks."

Blade's head snapped toward Marcus's younger brother, eyes going wide at the suggestion.

"Umm, would you guys mind stepping away from my crime scene?" Sheriff Burke said, stepping out of his vehicle and making his way toward the dead body. "It's hard to work up a story with you adding to the physical evidence."

The sheriff used his foot to kick dirt over the footprints surrounding the body.

"We only want one set of prints around the body. Makes an 'accident' much easier to support."

"I think it's time for us to leave, boys," Marcus ordered, picking up Lucas's knapsack and double-checking that they had not left any physical evidence of themselves around the crime scene. Burke would have to cover up their bike tracks as well before calling in forensics.

"I'll double-check again before I call this in," the sheriff added, watching Marcus as he attempted to kick dirt over some tracks.

"So, I guess that means no stabby-stabby," Blade

muttered, kissing his favorite blade before sliding it back into the harness attached to his belt.

"I didn't hear that," Burke called, bending down to examine the body. "Jesus Christ. You really did a number on this guy, kid."

Caden felt Lucas tense beside him. He kept his arm wrapped around Lucas's shoulder and pulled him closer to his body.

He loved this dude and would always be there to love and protect him—even when it was clear that Lucas didn't need anyone protecting him.

The guys all jumped onto their motorcycles, with Lucas wrapping his arms firmly around Caden's stomach. His body fit perfectly behind Caden on his bike—like the spot was made just for him.

"Ready?" Caden asked, squeezing Lucas's hand.

"Always," Lucas replied, leaning forward and kissing Caden's back.

God, he loved this man.

30

CADEN

"Oh yeah. Right there," Caden moaned, tilting his head back and giving in to the pleasures of Lucas's mouth.

The dude had been sucking on his balls for the last fifteen minutes, and he swore he was so close to busting his fuckin' load.

"Mmm," the boy groaned from somewhere down between his legs.

Caden had given over all control and was currently at the mercy of the demon's wicked tongue.

"I love how your cock gets harder every time I drag my tongue across your balls."

"I'll be honest. I've never had anyone suck on my nuts quite like you. I swear, you've got a magical tongue." Caden lifted his head to glance down at the chestnut eyes currently gleaming at him right next to his dick. Talk about a fucking sexy sight. "You're so fucking beautiful down there."

Lucas smiled. He did that a lot lately.

It had been three weeks since the incident with Lucas's ex, and the investigation had officially been closed.

There were a few questions as to why his ex had come searching for him in New Mexico, but once everyone realized this was a case of domestic violence, they quickly backed off and closed the case as a death by accident.

Not that any of them really cared about the investigation. No jury in their right mind would ever convict someone who murdered their abuser in self-defense.

Ever since that night, Lucas never stopped smiling. And Caden never stopped coming.

They had been fucking like rabbits. It was kind of getting concerning. Caden wasn't quite sure how much more fluids he had in him, but he wasn't willing to tell the boy between his legs no. No red-blooded man would ever turn down a sexy-ass dude on his knees, willing to suck his dick. Or lick his balls. Or let him fuck his ass. Or eat his ass.

That last one had been a surprise to Caden. In all his sexually active years, he had never once had his ass eaten until Lucas surprised him one night in the shower. Ho...ly... shit. How come nobody ever told guys how good it was to get your ass eaten? It was like discovering a second cum trigger! Let's just say that getting his ass eaten was now on their regular rotation.

The sound of foil being torn open caught Caden's attention.

His dick got harder.

He watched as Lucas rolled a condom onto his cock before slicking it up with lube.

"I want you to fuck me till I can't remember my name," Lucas ordered with heated eyes that never left his.

"Hell yeah!" Caden exclaimed, swinging his leg over the boy's head and leaping off the bed with excitement.

He grabbed Lucas's hips and pulled them down over the edge of the bed. Now it was his turn to drive his boy wild.

As Caden had pleasantly discovered, Lucas's favorite position happened to be doggy style. He loved being dominated and aggressively pounded to the point where he lost all control and was at the mercy of Caden's dominance.

The boy had a thing for aggressive men controlling him while in the bedroom—within reason, of course. There was a fine line between dominance and abuse. And Caden was all about the dominance.

Lining up his cock with Lucas's perfect pink hole, he took a moment to appreciate the majestic sight before him. Somehow, this gorgeous creature had decided to fall in love with him. To give him access to such a magnificent body anytime he wanted.

"God, you're so fucking gorgeous," Caden said once more. It was important that Lucas knew just how special he was to him. He just couldn't help himself.

A captivating smile gazed back at him from over Lucas's shoulder.

"Right back at ya, stud."

"You ready for this dick?" Caden asked, slapping his thick piece of meat a few times against Lucas's perky little butt. He loved the thick flopping sound his cock made as it slapped against his cheeks.

"I've been ready for it all morning." Lucas moaned, arching his back just the way Caden loved.

Lining up his dick once again, Caden pushed forward, groaning as Lucas's tight hole opened for him.

He carefully slid in, giving his boy time to adjust to the size of his meat.

"Fuck, babe." Lucas groaned, slowly pressing his ass back until it was flush against Caden's abdomen. "God, I love that dick."

Gripping the sides of Lucas's hips, he waited, loving the warm heat surrounding his meat.

"Hold on to something," Caden warned. He loved the tiny whimper that escaped Lucas's lips as he waited impatiently for his pounding to begin.

With that, Caden tightened his grip and began to fuck into his boy. He started slowly at first, giving the boy's hole a chance to adjust before quickly building to a pace that had Lucas gasping and grunting.

Snapping his hips forward, he drove in hard and quick, then slow and deep, changing it up to keep Lucas on his toes.

The sounds spilling from Lucas's lips were sinful. The boy loved to moan and talk dirty and never shied away from telling Caden exactly what he wanted and how hard he wanted it.

Sweat dripping down his chiseled chest, Caden growled as he pounded hard into his boy.

"Oh yes! Harder. Right there! Fuck yes." The words spilled from Lucas's mouth without any rhyme or reason.

He watched as his dick disappeared between Lucas's perfectly round ass cheeks. *Fuck, the man was gorgeous, taking his dick*. It was like his cock was meant to be buried deep inside the horny twenty-four-year-old, who kept Caden gasping and begging for more.

"Are you close?" Caden huffed, feeling his balls tighten and realizing he was just about to bust.

"Fuck. Yes," the boy choked out before jerking his head back and letting out a wicked cry.

Caden could feel Lucas's hole tighten around his dick as Lucas came all over the bedsheet beneath him. Feeling his boy come on his cock sent Caden over the edge as well.

He unloaded into Lucas's ass, drilling him hard, hoping to ride out the boy's orgasm for as long as possible.

The feeling was amazing—Lucas's hole constricting around his throbbing cock as they both came together, a sweaty pile of horny man-dudes.

Once they both stopped spasming, Caden fell onto Lucas's body, draping him in sweat and muscle.

"Fuck. I love feeling your weight on me and your dick deep inside me." Lucas moaned, his face muffled by the bed beneath him.

"I love feeling you beneath me," Caden responded, leaning forward and gently kissing his neck. "You're so fucking amazing."

Lucas began to chuckle. "Your dick is amazing."

Too tired to bother lifting his head, he laid it down

against Lucas's back and reminded him, "Hey, I'm more than just a dick."

Lucas intertwined their fingers together along the mattress. "Yes, you're sweet, loving, a great father, and the most closeted romantic I have ever met."

Caden chuckled. "Hey, I think the candles help set the mood."

"They do. And I love them. And I can't wait to tell Ace how you set the mood, then railed me hard all before Alexis's wedding."

"Evil. That's what you are."

Lucas pulled Caden's arms close around his chest.

He loved it when the boy made him feel like his one and only protector.

The truth was, Lucas didn't need protecting; he just wanted to feel loved and safe. And Caden was more than happy to give him both.

"I love you, Cade."

"Love you, too, Luc. We should probably get up and get ready for Alexis and Jake's wedding though."

"Argh. I have no idea how I'm going to walk. I think you broke my ass."

31

LUCAS

*Y*up. His ass was definitely broken.

It had been two hours since Caden's dicking of a lifetime, and Lucas swore he could still feel the man's cock inside him.

Concentrate. There is a classy wedding taking place, and here you are, thinking about that monster meat you had mashing up your insides.

Classy?

They were seated in the second to last row, with Lizzy squeezed in between them, watching an ex-stripper marry the town horndog.

Was it classy? Well, it was classy by Shadow Viper crew standards. The venue they had chosen was the large park in the middle of town. It was free, spacious, and accessible to all the townsfolk who were invited... which was pretty much everyone.

Ace and Lucas had spiced up the joint by adding satin

ribbons and flowers galore. Apparently, the gay decorating gene was strong in Marcus's little brother.

Listening to Ace order flowers on the phone and then threaten to stab the owner in the eye if they did not give him a fifty percent discount was entertaining as fuck. Thankfully, the florist was a town over, so threatening his demise would not capture the sheriff's attention.

Sitting in the folding chairs provided by the local high school and decorated by the drama club, Lucas listened to the classical music playing over the speakers that Marcus generously donated. It was strange hearing violins and pianos playing when the happy couple to be wed normally listened to rock music and exotic pop. He figured Alexis was really trying to class it up for her wedding.

Wrapping his arm around his daughter and Lucas, Caden leaned over and gently caressed Lucas's shoulder. It was a small gesture, but it really meant the world to him.

As with every biker wedding, the guests in attendance decided to party hard after the nuptials were exchanged. Whiskey and beer were consumed in high volumes, while champagne and martinis were consumed by the gay squad; current members included Ace and Lucas, and even Bobby was in attendance. Caden refused to drink the martini Lucas offered him, claiming that he had balls and the pansy drink would never touch his lips.

Lucas reminded him that if he ever wanted his pansy lips to ever suck his cock again, he would have to chug the martini, then fuck him later in the bathroom stall.

The martini disappeared.

It was just after nine p.m. when Alexis and Jake finally performed their waltz in front of everyone. To say that people's mouths hit the floor when Jake began following Alexis's lead was putting it mildly.

They actually weren't half bad. Lucas figured that with a few more sessions, the two would be able to dance without stepping on each other's toes and without Jake trying to hump Alexis's leg like a horny stray dog.

"Hey, bud," Marcus said, slapping Lucas on the back and interrupting a conversation he was having with Cade. "I wanted to introduce you to Ms. Kathy Chermain. She's the director of social planning working directly for the mayor."

"It's nice to meet you, Luc," a short, plump woman with rosy cheeks and a gentle smile greeted. Ms. Chermain was exactly how Lucas would have pictured Mrs. Claus if she were a real woman. "I've heard a lot about you and was dying to meet you."

"Oh, it's a pleasure to meet you, Ms. Chermain." Lucas stepped forward and shook her hand. He had never heard of the woman before, so he had no idea why she was so interested in him.

"I was told that you helped teach and train Alexis and Jake with their performance here tonight."

Lucas's cheeks flushed. He wasn't sure if Ms. Chermain was going to give him a compliment or a scolding.

"Well, yes, I..."

"I loved it!" the woman said, clapping her hands on her knees and bending over all excited. "I also saw that YouTube video of you singing in the bar and can't believe you aren't on Broadway."

A huge smile spread across Lucas's face when he realized that she was a fan and not the talent police, come to arrest him for crimes against dance and music.

"Well, thank you! I went to college to study musical theater and love to perform."

"Well, that's exactly why I'm here."

Lucas looked up at Caden, who had his arm around his waist, being the amazing supporting boyfriend he always was.

"I'd like to put together a performing arts program for the town. Dance, theater, painting. And I was hoping that I could hire you to design and teach the dance and theater programs. It would just be part-time at the beginning until we determine if there's an interest in the programs, but so far, everyone I have talked to would be thrilled to place their child in a program designed and taught by you!"

Lucas's mouth fell open. Was she being for real?

"Seriously? Me? But... I..."

"But nothing. You are majorly talented, and we have all seen your moves online," Marcus cut in. "I've already spoken with Ms. Chermain, and it sounds like the program would not interfere with your job at the bar. Plus, I was going to switch up your duties anyway. You've proven that you are good at thinking on your feet, so I want to use your talents for *other* things," Marcus explained.

Wow, the opportunity to design and teach a program that he loved? It was a perfect opportunity.

"I think you should do it, babe," Cade said beside him,

tightening his grip on his waist. "You love to sing and dance, plus the kids love you, and you know that Lizzy would be the first to sign up for your classes."

He was right. It sounded like an amazing opportunity, plus he could still keep working at the bar with Cade and all his friends as well. Lucas didn't want to admit it, but he loved working with Cade and being so close to him every single day.

Lucas smiled and stuck out his hand.

"I'd love to, Ms. Chermain."

With that, Marcus and Ms. Chermain walked away, heading toward the bride and groom to join them in a few shots, no doubt. In this town, even the director of social planning was always willing to get down for a good time.

"Shall we dance?" Caden asked, holding out his hand and waiting for Lucas to take it.

"What? Seriously?" Lucas asked, shocked by the man's request. "Whatever happened to you having balls and stuff?"

Caden chuckled. "Oh, I still have those. They've just decided to make a deal with my heart that if they allow me to participate in this most romantic of acts, they will get to spend the night balls deep in that ass of yours. Of course, my heart accepted the deal."

"Of course it did," Lucas answered with a chuckle of his own. While Caden liked to play all tough and macho on the outside, on the inside, he was all gooey and loveable. Somehow, Lucas had found that rough and possessive man, who fucked like a stallion, but also had a heart of gold.

Yes, his fantasy man really did exist. He just had to date an evil monster first to find him.

Taking Caden's hand, he led the love of his life to the section of the park where everyone was dancing. They slid in next to Ace, who was dancing with Bobby, of all people.

"Please tell me that this isn't a thing now," Lucas asked Ace and Bobby.

Ace rolled his eyes.

"Not a chance. Ace is just using me to make some dude jealous, but he won't tell me who. My money's on Biker Daddy over there," Bobby answered, nodding over to where an older gentleman in his late fifties was standing next to a tree, holding a beer.

Lucas shook his head. He highly doubted that man was who Ace was trying to make jealous. Ace was a pretty confident guy. If he really wanted that man, he would have simply walked up to him and asked him.

No, Ace was trying to make someone else jealous who he was afraid to approach. Someone he wasn't sure might be interested in him... Someone like...

Lucas followed Ace's gaze over to the far east side of the park, where a bunch of guys from the crew were taking shots at the bar. There were three men gathered in the group, but only one kept glancing over in Ace's direction.

No. Fuckin'. Way.

Ace's eyes quickly diverted when Blade's head turned in his direction.

Lucas grinned at Ace when the man finally looked his

way. They exchanged a knowing glance and immediately understood.

"I'm sure whoever it is will be under Ace's spell in no time," Lucas noted. "Now, I'd like to dance with my hot-as-fuck boyfriend, so see you losers later." Lucas pulled Caden a few feet away and threw his arms over his man's shoulders.

"It's about time I finally got you all to myself," Caden whispered, pulling Lucas's body firmly against his and showing him just how hard he really was at the moment.

"Jesus, man. A rod like that can injure someone if you aren't careful."

"The only thing I'm interested in injuring is that prostate of yours when we get home."

"You know how much I love it when you talk dirty to me. What time is Lizzy being picked up?"

"Her mom picked her up an hour ago, so it's just you and me for the remainder of the wedding."

A wicked grin spread across Lucas's face.

"Then, how about we slip away, and you get started with that assault on my prostate," Lucas suggested, knowing full well what the answer would be.

"God, I love it when you speak my love language." Caden chuckled as he grabbed Lucas's hand and quickly led him through the crowd of drunken bikers taking advantage of the open bar.

Somehow, this had become Lucas's life. He had met the man of his dreams while escaping the man of his nightmares.

Stopping quickly, Lucas pulled Caden's body into his. They both stared at each other with such love in their eyes.

"What's wrong?" Caden asked, love turning into concern, the longer they stood there.

"Nothing. I just really wanted to kiss you," Lucas said, standing up on his toes and locking lips with the sexiest man he had ever met.

They kissed long and deep under a blanket of late summer stars.

Somehow, he had managed to score the perfect balance of rough biker dude and sweetheart romantic.

God, he loved this man.

The End

ABOUT THE AUTHOR

Matthew Dante is a Canadian author who writes LGBTQ+ Dark Romances and Thrillers. He graduated with a Major in Criminology and has been working in the financial crimes industry for over twenty years. He is an avid reader, world traveler, lover of all things Marvel and DC, and a romantic at heart.

As an author, your reviews are very important as these provide potential readers with a reason to give our books a try. So, if you enjoyed reading this book or others, please consider taking a few moments to leave a review.

To stay up to date on all of Matthew Dante's workings, consider joining his newsletter and following him on all his social media platforms. Also, check out his website at matthewdante.com.

ACKNOWLEDGMENTS

I want to take a moment to thank you, my amazing readers. Without your love, support, and enthusiasm, none of these stories would have ever been written. You can't imagine how wonderful it feels to receive a message from someone who has just finished reading my book and can't wait for the next one to be released. These simple words have a tremendous effect on us authors. It is this excitement and love that drives us to work tirelessly to create the perfect story that we all hope you will love.

Also, I wanted to thank my wonderful family, who keeps me smiling and is always happy to listen to me freak out or complain when I am stuck on a story arc. Your words of wisdom always help me see the brighter side of things.

Now it's time for Book 2! Stay tuned for more details and teasers.

BOOKS BY MATTHEW DANTE

MM Dark Romance

FRACTURED SERIES

Fractured Love (Book 1)

Fractured Mind (Book 2)

Fractured Soul (Book 3)

ROUGH EDGES

Laying Claim (Book 1)

Protecting His (Book 2)

Devouring Sin (Book 3)

Avenging Des (Book 4)

Defending You (Book 5)

Obeying Orders (Book 6)

BOOK OF SIN

The Collector (Book 1)

The Broker (Book 2)

The Chameleon (Book 3)

The Chemist (Book 4)

BOOKS BY MATTHEW DANTE

BIKERS OF MAYHEM

Primal Urges (Book 1)

As I Say...

The Naughty List

MM Romance

Love to Hate You

The Devil Wears Pink

A Campfire Confession (Packing: An MM Anthology)